Laura is determined to avoid Graham, but her heart keeps betraying her.

"Laura, honey, are you hurt?"

Laura shook her head and wiped away her tears with the back of her hand. Graham reached down and gently lifted her to her feet. His gray eyes anxiously searched her face.

"You're late," she sniffled.

Graham looked bewildered. "Late?"

Laura nodded and turned a tear-streaked face to him. "You're supposed to rescue me before I get in trouble, not after." She offered him a weak smile.

Graham groaned softly and drew her to his chest, enveloping her in the protective circle of his strong arms. He stroked her hair tenderly. Laura leaned against him, the soft denim of his shirt caressing her cheek. The steady beat of his heart matched her own, and she sighed contentedly. This was the second time in two days that she'd found herself cradled in his arms, and it felt so right.

Her conscience reminded her Graham belonged to another, but she did not release him. Instead, she snuggled against him more closely, her arms wrapping around his waist. *Just a minute more,* she told herself, *I need to be held just a minute more.*

NANCY LAVO is a gifted author from the big state of Texas where she lives with her husband and three children. *A Change of Heart* is Nancy's first inspirational romance.

A Change of Heart

Nancy Lavo

Heartsong Presents

To God be the glory!

A note from the Author:
*I love to hear from my readers! You may write to me at
the following address:* **Nancy Lavo
Author Relations
P.O. Box 719
Uhrichsville, OH 44683**

ISBN 1-55748-702-2

A CHANGE OF HEART

Cover illustration by Gary Maria.

PRINTED IN THE U.S.A.

one

Laura slumped at her desk, stunned, her hand still resting on the telephone receiver. She stared unseeing through the chintz-framed window before her.

"He can't go," she whispered desolately. "I can't believe it. He really can't go."

The stack of travel brochures she had pored over so lovingly for six months caught her eye. Just looking at them made her furious. With an angry sweep of her hand, she dashed the pile to the floor.

"It's all your fault," she berated the scattered pages. "All those promises about a week to remember and life-changing vacations. I believed you! I counted on you! And now he can't go!"

Actually, you are the one to blame, her little voice from within accused. *Haven't you learned? You can't depend on anyone but yourself. The others will abandon you. They always do. And you'll be the one hurt.* The little voice delivered its cruel barbs with its usual efficiency.

Laura winced as the pain drove through her like a knife. *Pain.* That was it exactly. And she'd thought herself immune to pain.

That immunity had been carefully cultivated over the last nine years through her strict policy of cool detachment. She had become an observer of life, no longer an active participant. Life was too risky. Her heart was too vulnerable.

Her best defense had been a pleasant, although impenetrable exterior. No one could get close enough to hurt her.

Planning this vacation with her father and best friend, allowing herself to hope and dream, was the first time she could remember permitting her armor to slip. And the penalty was the same, pain. The little voice persisted, *Never drop your defenses; never let your heart get involved.*

Even now, Laura wasn't sure why she felt such an urgency about this cruise with her father. Maybe it was the realization that after this week, her time would no longer be her own. Once she began as an accountant with Cunningham and Associates, she doubted that between her busy schedule and her father's, there would be any free time to spend together.

Laura secretly hoped a week together would help them forge a close relationship, like the one she had abandoned years ago.

Or maybe she just needed to know she had some direction as she plunged into adult life.

Laura nodded absently in confirmation. All that was true. But there was more. The nagging void within Laura, her constant companion for nine long years, had suddenly become too painful to bear. Her self-imposed isolation was taking its toll on her. Overwhelming loneliness crushed in around her, draining Laura of her desire to live. Something had to change before it was too late. And Laura was ready to try.

She had a plan. The plan was unique in that it would marked the first time Laura had acted in open rebellion to the bitter tyrant that dominated her life, her little voice.

Her plan was simple. Once she and her father were at sea, a neutral location without painful memories tied to it from the past, she would pour out her heart to him. She'd apologize for shutting him out, she'd explain she was willing to risk opening up, and she'd beg him to show her how. She sensed he had the power to help her move forward with her life.

It had seemed so close at hand that a tiny spark of hope had ignited within her heart. At least until she had learned her father couldn't go.

Laura sighed deeply. A tear trickled unnoticed down her smooth cheek. "Oh Daddy," she whispered to the empty room. "I'm so lonely and afraid. I need you. Help me make some sense of my life." The tears flowed freely now, and for the first time in a long time, she allowed herself the luxury of a good cry.

❧

"Okay," Kathi began breathlessly, after bursting through the front door and bounding up the stairs two at a time. "What exactly did your father say?"

She had come immediately to Laura's home at the urgent request of her best friend. The sight of Laura's red-rimmed eyes and tear-streaked face confirmed the gravity of the situation. Laura wasn't one to cry over petty troubles. In fact, Laura wasn't one to cry at all.

Kathi crossed the room, stepping over the pile of glossy travel brochures and snuggled into an overstuffed chair beside her friend. She positioned her arms on the armrest of the chair, visibly bracing herself for the worst. "Well?"

A slight smile tugged at the corner of Laura's mouth as she considered her guest. Kathi Davis had been her best friend since the second grade. After Laura's mother had died, Kathi had been her only friend.

As far as Laura could tell, they were total opposites, physically and philosophically. Kathi was petite and curvaceous, even a bit voluptuous, with a shock of dark, curly hair and the bluest eyes Laura had ever seen. Laura categorized herself as a tall, skinny, dishwater blond with boring brown eyes.

Kathi found life funny and exciting, while Laura approached it with clinical detachment. *Total opposites. Yet,* Laura thought affectionately, *I couldn't ask for a more wonderful companion.*

Kathi never asked for more than Laura could give, never tried to delve too deeply into Laura's innermost thoughts. Laura suspected the fact that Kathi was not a deep thinker had much to do with the superficial nature of their friendship, and frankly, up until now, that was all Laura wanted.

Laura's smile faded as her thoughts drifted back to Kathi's question. "He said he couldn't make the cruise. He's been called to chair some banking committee delegation in Munich the same week as our trip." Laura's voice quavered as she continued, "He told me he's sorry; it's unavoidable; and he'll make it up to us."

"Oh, Laura." Kathi jumped to her feet and embraced her tightly. "I just know he would prefer to go and spend time with you. . .Let me think. . .I know! We can postpone the trip!"

Laura shook her head. "No good, not with such short notice. We'd have to forfeit our tickets."

"Oh." Kathi hesitated a moment, groping to find the right words of comfort. She placed her hands on Laura's shoulders. "Hey," she said softly, her blue eyes searching Laura's face, "I know I'm not your dad, but we'll be together, just you and me, and I know we'll have a terrific time, like always. You'll see."

Laura stepped back, deeply embarrassed to be so emotional. She considered it a sign of weakness. And she couldn't be weak. Weak people get hurt.

She spoke with forced enthusiasm. "You're right. We will have a wonderful time. But we won't be alone. I forgot to mention Dad is sending someone along in his place."

"What do you mean he's sending someone in his place?" Kathi eyed her quizzically. "What are you talking about?"

Laura shrugged. "I don't know most of the details, but Dad mentioned that a friend of his would accompany us—as a kind of chaperone, I guess."

"A chaperone?" Kathi dropped dejectedly into her chair. "Some crotchety, old woman he works with, no doubt."

"No doubt."

"And she'll make us go to bed at 9:00 and play shuffleboard and attend lectures, and. . ."

"Okay, Okay, I've got the picture." Laura grimaced. "Hopefully, you're wrong. Anyway, we won't know for sure until I talk to Dad. We're having dinner tonight. A combination graduation and bon voyage celebration. I'll get the low down on her then."

Kathi groaned. "I am thoroughly depressed." Her bright smile belied the truth of her words. "I guess there's only one thing to do."

Laura eyed her suspiciously. "And what would that be?"

"Why, shop, of course! Haven't you ever heard of therapeutic shopping? It's a guaranteed cure for depression!"

Laura shook her head in mock exasperation. "Kathi, you are too much! You know I hate to shop, and I know you already have more clothes packed than you could wear on two cruises!"

Kathi smiled wickedly. "True, true. However, I saw the most beautiful pair of sandals at Bolton's last week. At the time, I thought they were too expensive." Kathi placed her hand dramatically over her heart. "But, with this distressing turn of events, I feel they'll be just what the doctor ordered!"

Laura opened her mouth to protest, "I don't. . ."

Kathi interrupted, shaking her head. "I won't take no for an answer. You've got to get over this unnatural aversion to shopping. It's a woman's God-given privilege. Anyway, after the cruise, you won't have time for shopping. You'll be too busy being a stuffy old accountant." She started for the door. In a voice that would tolerate no dissension she added, "I've got my car outside, we'll take it."

Laura raised her arms in surrender. "Okay, okay, I give up. Once again, I've let you bully me into something." She smiled as she grabbed her purse off the desk and headed down the stairs. "By the way," she called after her retreating friend. "What did you mean by a stuffy, old accountant?"

No answer. Laura tried again. "Come on, I'm serious. Do you really think I'm stuffy?"

Unrepentant giggles drifted up the stairs, giving Laura her answer.

two

"Laura, you look lovely tonight." Howard Wells beamed at his daughter across the linen covered table. *She has her mother's refined look,* he thought approvingly, high, *sculpted cheekbones, a tiny straight nose and a rosy Cupid's bow mouth.* But it was her eyes, of the deepest brown velvet, heavily fringed with long brown lashes that most reminded him of his beloved wife.

Laura looked especially lovely in the candlelight, he thought, with her thick mane of honey gold hair twisted into an elaborate knot at the nape of her neck. Her white silk dress, though characteristically simple, highlighted her classic beauty.

"You've grown into a lovely young woman while my back has been turned." His voice faltered slightly as Laura offered him a smile.

When she smiled, he mused, if you didn't look too closely at the guarded expression in her eyes, you could almost forget the past.

Howard summoned a favorite memory: one of his wife Lynn and daughter Laura giggling together over some secret joke. They'd be sitting side by side, golden heads together, hands lovingly entwined. He smiled at the recollection.

They were so much a part of each other, mother and daughter appeared to function as one. They looked alike, smiled alike, talked alike, and Howard would swear to this day, even their thoughts were synchronized. During Laura's difficult preteen years, when most girls spurned the friendship of their mothers, Laura and Lynn had remained the closest of friends.

A black cloud settled over the memory, and the picture changed. Lynn was gone, dead from a cancer that stole her young life, almost without warning. Gone too was the laughing, golden-haired daughter. In her place was a somber-eyed girl. Grief, more powerful than any consolation he could provide, had left her bereft.

He watched over the ensuing months as Laura built a carefully constructed wall around her emotions, forbidding access to her devastated heart. She wouldn't risk losing that much again.

A familiar guilt tugged at Howard's heart. He knew he had let her down. In her grief, he'd offered no hope. He hadn't had any to offer. Over time, a cavernous gulf had formed between father and daughter as Laura had retreated into the safety of isolation and Howard had limped along in his own grief.

Now, years later, he'd found the answer. He'd found hope. And today, as he studied his beautiful daughter, he felt an urgency to share it with her. If only he knew how. If only she'd listen.

Laura regarded her distinguished father sitting across from her and seriously considered going ahead with her plan tonight and pouring out her troubled heart to him. But she hesitated. The plan, hatched in the protected recesses of her mind, looked flimsy in the glaring light of reality.

They were such strangers now. After all the years they had spent avoiding their true feelings, she was afraid. What if he didn't understand what she was trying to say, or worse, what if he didn't care?

Don't risk it, her little voice warned. *You'll get hurt. Don't let him get close. You don't need anyone.*

Howard was unaware of the battle raging within her as she sat sedately before him. Should she take the chance and open up to him, possibly finding the solution to her loneliness, or should she remain silent, and bear her burden alone?

Ultimately, it was fear, her fear of rejection and pain, that won out, and she dismissed the plan as futile.

"So how does it feel to have an accountant in the family?" Laura broke the uncomfortable silence with a neutral subject. "Are you feeling a little threatened with a financial wizard for a daughter?"

Howard's loud burst of laughter echoed across the quiet dining room, drawing several curious stares. "Laura, honey, I couldn't be prouder!" He leaned across the table to emphasize his words.

"Of course, the way I figure it, you couldn't help but be a financial genius—what with me for your old man!"

"Oh you," Laura countered with a laugh. "I hope I didn't inherit your ego."

"Touché. Oh, by the way." Howard fumbled in his coat pocket. "I've got a little something here for you." He produced a small rectangular box, richly wrapped in gold paper and tied up with white ribbon.

"Now, Dad," Laura chided. "You didn't need to get me anything else. My goodness, the new luggage and the cruise are more than enough."

"It's not every day a father can celebrate his daughter's graduation from college, magna cum laude no less. I thought you deserved a little something extra." He handed the package to Laura. "Besides, it's not new."

"Oh?" Laura's eyes bespoke her confusion.

Howard nodded toward the package in her hand, indicating she would understand when she opened it. Laura slipped the ribbon from the box, then tore the gold paper away. The black velvet box inside looked vaguely familiar. She opened the lid gingerly, then gasped.

"It was your mom's," Howard confirmed, anxiously watching her expression. "She always wanted you to have it. We decided to wait until you graduated to give it to you."

Laura cradled the box reverently. "It's beautiful," she whispered. "Even more beautiful than I remembered."

Inside was a heavy gold bracelet composed of connecting gold links. Each square link was set with a diamond weighing a quarter of a carat. The diamonds were mounted flush within the link, giving the bracelet a smooth, sleek appearance.

Laura lifted it from the box. "Just look how it sparkles." Mesmerized, she turned the bracelet from side to side, watching the brilliant gems catch the light. "It's really too valuable to wear." She started to return it to the box.

"Nonsense," Howard replied. "I've waited all this time to see you wear it. And you will!" He reached across the table, retrieved the bracelet from the box and laid it gently across her small wrist.

"See here?" he asked, indicating the catch with his finger. "I had the jeweler install a special safety latch on it. You couldn't lose it if you wanted to." He smiled warmly at his daughter. "I want you to wear it, honey. Life's just too short. . ." his voice trailed off.

Laura felt tears stinging her eyes. Before they could fall and expose her vulnerability, however, the waiter appeared with their food. She was thankful for the reprieve. By diverting her attention to the plate before her, she was able to regain her flagging composure.

Dinner smelled delicious. Thick, grilled steaks and fluffy, baked potatoes waited temptingly on the plates before them. They busied themselves eating, and it was several minutes before either spoke.

"Will you and Kathi be ready to go first thing tomorrow? It'd be best to have your suitcases ready to go tonight—that way we'll avoid any problems in the morning."

Laura smiled, her brown eyes bright with amusement. "The suitcases are the problem! Well, at least to Kathi they are."

Howard's obvious confusion added to her amusement. "Until I mentioned the two-hundred-pound-luggage limit to Kathi this afternoon, she was planning to bring her entire wardrobe." Laura chuckled at the memory of her best friend trying frantically to decide which pairs of shoes, of the twenty some pairs she had packed, she would be willing to leave behind.

"Mercy!" Howard exclaimed. "The brochures were very explicit on the luggage restrictions. Of course, I don't suppose Kathi took the time to read them." He stabbed the air with his fork to punctuate his words. "Frankly, I don't believe that child has any sense at all. Certainly, two hundred pounds of clothing should be enough for one week."

"I was finally able to convince her of that. However, at this point, I think she is considering packing in plastic trash bags to save the six or seven pounds her suitcases weigh!" Laura added mischievously.

Howard shook his head in dismay. "I can see I was wise in finding a replacement for myself for the cruise. You girls are in definite need of a caretaker."

Laura laid down her fork and looked at her father. "You haven't told me who our chaperone will be."

"Haven't I? No, I guess I haven't. Sorry, honey, with all the rush to finalize my plans, I simply forgot." Howard smiled apologetically.

Laura toyed with her new bracelet as she waited patiently for his reply. After several seconds of silence, she prompted him, "Well, who is she?"

"She? Oh no, honey, it's a he. Good friend of mine, Graham Kirkland."

"Graham Kirkland?" Laura repeated incredulously. "Not the Graham Kirkland from down the street?"

"Yes, he's the one," Howard admitted with pride, "though he doesn't live there anymore. He's got his own place now."

"Dad!" Laura's voice rose in alarm. "You can't mean it. You are actually sending Graham Kirkland on a week long cruise with Kathi and me?"

"Yes." Howard's puzzled expression indicated he had no idea why that information should upset his daughter. "Is there a problem?"

"Yes, there's a problem. He's horrible!"

"Laura," her father chastised with the tone of voice one usually uses to reprimand young children, "Graham is a fine, responsible young man who was kind enough to volunteer to escort you girls when I found I had to be in Munich."

"A fine young man?" Laura repeated in disbelief. "Dad, he's . . .he's gross." The minute the words were out of her mouth she berated herself for her childish description. She hadn't used the word gross since the fifth grade. *Yet,* she thought wryly, *it was certainly succinct in Graham's case. It might even be too generous.*

Seeing her father's bewilderment, Laura went on to clarify her position. "Dad, Graham is a social misfit. He is what we refer to as a nerd."

Howard threw back his head and roared laughter. "A nerd! Now that's a word I don't hear very often. And when did you last see this. . .this nerd, Laura?"

Laura found her father's amusement at her expense annoying. "I don't know," she answered defensively, twisting the gold bracelet on her wrist with a vengeance. "At my high school graduation party, I think."

She paused for a moment to consider. "Yes, that's it, I'm sure. There were several alumni there, and Graham was one of them. He stood in a corner the entire evening and gawked." Laura grimaced as her memory sharpened. "He's real tall, seven feet at least, and real skinny—all legs and arms, and a mouthful of braces."

Laura turned pleading eyes to her father. "Dad, you can't do this. Graham's such a nerd, he'll ruin the entire cruise." She shuddered for emphasis.

Howard was unmoved by his daughter's obvious exaggerations. "That was over four years ago, Laura. Isn't it possible he's changed?"

"Changed? Sure, it's possible." Skepticism was heavy in her voice. "But it would take a miracle to change him into something decent. And, we both know there are no such things as miracles."

Deciding to let that comment pass, Howard laughed, his eyes twinkling with mirth. "Be that as it may, Laura, the ship sails tomorrow afternoon, and Graham will be on it. I, for one, think he's the perfect choice for a companion."

"Perfect choice for an anchor, you mean," Laura mumbled ungraciously.

Howard chose not to respond to her remark. Laura could see that her father was genuinely delighted with this intolerable situation, and she struggled to find the best approach to take to dissuade him from sending Graham.

Maybe she could cast doubts on Graham's reputation. Surely, her father wouldn't want her traveling with someone of questionable morals.

"So, just how did you get involved with Graham Kirkland?" Her nose wrinkled in distaste at the mention of his name. "I mean, what do you know about him. . .his character? I can't imagine he would make a suitable chaperone for two single women."

Her father smiled broadly, as if he had anticipated her question. "Graham and I attend church together, a men's Bible study actually."

Laura laughed merrily. "Now that's funny; but no, really, I'm serious. Where did you dig him up? Let's face it; he's not exactly the kind of guy you'd seek out for company, and frankly," she leaned across the table and whispered conspiratorially, "since we know so little about him, I think it would be best for Kathi and I to sail alone."

Howard Wells studied his daughter for several moments before he spoke. When he did speak, his voice was slow and deliberate. "I'm not kidding. Graham and I have been going to the Bible study for almost a year now. And I am very well acquainted with Graham. He's a great guy, with the highest moral standards, and I place you girls in his hands with the greatest confidence."

Howard stopped, allowing his words to sink in and waiting to see her reaction. Defiance was written plainly across her face. He wanted to discuss this delicate matter at just the right moment, certainly not in anger, but seeing there was no way out, he plunged along recklessly. "Graham has taught me a lot about our loving God." Howard paused, to take a deep breath. "And how important it is to make Him a part of our lives."

Laura's dark eyes flashed in indignation. She ground out bitterly, "Loving God? Ha! How can you even say that? I saw how much He loved Mom. That was swell of Him to let her suffer and die from cancer. And she liked Him!"

Laura was rigid in her chair, her hands tightly fisted on the table, the lovely features of her face now hardened in anger.

Almost immediately, she regretted becoming so emotional with her father. *You're weak,* her little voice taunted. *And the weak get hurt.*

Laura paused for a moment to cool off, glancing around the

darkened room, noting the way the flickering candlelight danced on each tabletop. Soft piano music drifted through the room. She hadn't noticed it until now. The effect was soothing, and she felt her anger melt away.

Once again in perfect control, she leveled her gaze on her father. "I'm sorry. That was uncalled for." Her voice was unmistakably cool. "This conversation has taken a turn for the worst. You and I have reached an impasse over Graham Kirkland, and since your mind is obviously made up, there is no need for further discussion. Since God is of no interest to me, I would prefer another topic, if you don't mind."

Howard sighed in resignation. He had known the subject was a touchy one, and ordinarily, he would have avoided such a confrontation at all costs, but he needed to tell her, and he had hoped perhaps tonight, she would listen. One look at her rigid frame, and the brittle gleam in her mahogany eyes told him she had not.

Disappointment was heavy in his voice as he said, "I am sorry you feel that way, Laura. About God and Graham. I had hoped you would hear me out." Seeing no softening in Laura's steely expression, he continued, "But I understand. And I'll drop it, for now."

The truce offered and accepted, both Laura and her father turned their attention to their dessert. The rich chocolate cake dripping with melted fudge, usually a favorite of both, did nothing to bolster their now ruined appetites, and neither seemed able to eat. An uncomfortable silence stretched between them.

Laura felt ungrateful. After all, her father had gone to the trouble of taking her out and her caustic words had spoiled the otherwise wonderful evening.

The little voice from within reminded her it was actually Howard's fault that the evening had been ruined. *If he hadn't cancelled out on the cruise and appointed that idiot Graham as chaperone,* the tyrant reasoned with its usual faulty logic, *the argument wouldn't have been necessary.*

Even so, Laura countered, *he is my father.* She looked at him across the table, and her heart filled with pity for him. He was obviously so disappointed. In an effort to repair the damage, she began to chatter, with an animation she did not feel, about her plans for her upcoming job.

Dutifully, Howard joined in, but both of them knew the previously amiable mood was lost.

After her father paid the bill, they stepped out of the restaurant into the late spring evening. The air had cooled slightly and a gentle breeze fragrant with the sweet perfume of honeysuckle caressed them. "Thanks for dinner, Dad. It was lovely."

Howard turned to face her, the evening shadows masking the raw emotion on his face. "You know, honey, I love you very much. In fact, you're all I've got. I know I've made a lot of mistakes with you in the past, but I'm doing the best I can to rectify them. Can you find it in your heart to forgive me? Can we be friends?"

Laura felt a tug at her heart. Hope flickered within her once again. He sounded so sincere. Maybe she could go through with her plan, once she got back from the cruise. She stood on tiptoe and pressed a kiss on his cheek. "I'd like that very much."

three

Sunday morning was a blur of activity. After a last-minute check that the luggage was secure and both tickets and traveler's checks were tucked safely in Laura's small leather purse, she and her father were on their way.

First stop was to pick up Kathi. She was standing on her front porch when they arrived, surrounded by a mountain of tapestry luggage. "I've already said my good-byes to Mother and Daddy," she began breathlessly, trying to drag several suitcases to the car. "Sorry, they aren't down to greet you, but anything before 10 A.M. around here is considered uncivilized." She shrugged. "You know how old people are." She giggled when she realized what she'd said to Mr. Wells. "Oops, present company excluded, of course." She giggled again.

Howard wasn't offended. He was accustomed to Kathi's habit of speaking first and thinking later. The many thoughtless remarks she had directed toward him over the years provided him with much amusement—and a profound sense of gratitude that she was someone else's daughter.

"Get in," he laughed, "and let this old man load up the car so we won't miss our planes." He surveyed her voluminous belongings with dismay. "Goodness, child, I hope you didn't forget anything."

Kathi missed the teasing tone of his voice and answered solemnly, "I hope so, too. That's absolutely all they will allow me to bring." She shook her head in resignation. "I'll just have to make do with what I have."

Laura caught her father's eye and silently warned him to stop this conversation, as it was obviously a sore spot for her friend. He winked his acknowledgement and with the luggage stowed snugly in the trunk, they were off.

"How do I look?" Kathi asked with a smile as Howard maneuvered the car out onto the deserted street.

She was dressed from head to toe in a bright, yellow jumpsuit and yellow espadrilles to match. Around her tiny wrist clattered six wooden bangles in various shades of tropical fruits. Enormous earrings, shaped like parrots, dangled from her earlobes to complete the exotic ensemble.

On anyone else, the outfit might be tacky, but on Kathi, Laura mused loyally, *it looks lovely.* "Kathi, I think you look wonderful. One glimpse of you, and I feel as though our vacation has already begun." She squeezed her friend's hand in approval.

Kathi stopped preening long enough to notice Laura's own attire, a navy linen suit with a white silk tee shirt and navy pumps, and shook her head in mild reproach. "Laura," she chided, "we are going to the Bahamas, not a board meeting."

"I'm comfortable in this," Laura replied a bit defensively. "Besides, I think it wise for young women traveling alone to look competent. No one will bother us."

Kathi was about to explain that she wanted to be bothered when she noticed Laura smoothing a strand of hair that had escaped from the chignon at the base of her neck. The diamond bracelet at her wrist caught the morning sun, and Kathi's attention was riveted to it.

"What is this?" She grabbed Laura's wrist to examine the bracelet. "It's gorgeous. Is it real? Can I borrow it? Where did you get it?" She fired off the questions so rapidly that Laura had no time to respond.

"It's a graduation present from her mother and I." Howard answered for his daughter. "It was her mother's."

"Oh." Kathi touched it reverently. "It's so beautiful. Valuable too, I'll bet. I definitely need to find a boyfriend to buy me nice stuff like that. Maybe there will be someone on the cruise." She was silent for the remainder of the trip, obviously strategizing just such a plan.

As the three of them stood at the gate after checking in with the airline, Laura and her father had their first opportunity to speak without interruption. Howard took her slender hand in his own and squeezed it gently. "I'll miss you."

Laura's reply was interrupted when the harried ticket agent announced the initial boarding for Miami-bound passengers. At the signal, the once lethargic crowd was instantly on its feet, grabbing their belongings and jockeying for position in line for the plane.

Howard hugged Kathi, who hopped around like an anxious schoolgirl, and teasingly admonished her to behave herself while on vacation. Her giggled response assured Howard her intentions were otherwise.

He turned to his daughter and embraced her tightly. "Have a wonderful time. I'm truly sorry I can't go with you." He drew back to look into Laura's soft brown eyes. "I'll make it up to you, I promise." He bent and gently kissed her forehead. "Have a safe trip. I love you."

The flight attendant called for the final boarding of passengers going to Miami and motioned for the girls to take their places on the plane. There was much Laura wanted to say to her father, but now, as they were being herded toward the plane, was not the time. Laura brushed a quick kiss on his cheek and reluctantly joined Kathi and the few passengers remaining to be boarded.

As an afterthought, Howard called out to them, "Girls, try to be tolerant of Graham." He paused for emphasis. "No matter what else, he is my friend."

Laura waved to signal her acknowledgement, and her father turned to leave. She heard the attendant call for the final boarding of first class passengers as she rounded the ramp. *Odd,* she thought, stepping inside the plane, *I could swear I just heard Dad laughing.*

≈

After the plane had leveled at its cruising altitude and the stewardesses had completed their discourse on airline safety regulations, Kathi spoke up. "Well, Laura my girl, we made it. It ought to be smooth sailing from here." She elbowed Laura playfully. "Get it? Smooth sailing?"

"Yes, you nut, I get it." Laura smiled indulgently at her friend, then returned her gaze to the view just outside her window. The plane cut effortlessly through the cottony-white landscape around them. "Can you believe we're finally leaving?" she voiced her thoughts aloud. "I've been looking forward to this for so long. . ." Her voice drifted off wistfully.

Kathi mistook her friend's remark to be one of enthusiasm and nodded, her dark curls shaking vigorously. "Me too! And I for one cannot wait to get started on my first shipboard romance. With one of those tall, dark, and handsome hunks they pictured in all the brochures." She smacked her lips in anticipation.

Laura rolled her eyes in amused tolerance. "I don't doubt that for a moment. I wonder if I shouldn't radio ahead and alert the captain about your reputation as a heartbreaker." She smiled into the guileless eyes of her companion. "I can only hope there will be enough men to satisfy you for an entire week."

Her voice was teasing, but there was an element of truth in what she'd said. Laura couldn't recall a time when Kathi had been without a boyfriend. Men flocked to her like moths to a flame. And, as she considered her friend beside her, she could certainly see why.

Kathi was lovely, but there was more. She was an eternal optimist. While she did not possess one of the great minds of the world, she did possess an unlimited supply of joy. *Something,* Laura thought longingly, *of which I am completely deficient.* It had been so long since she had experienced any emotion even faintly resembling joy, she was uncertain she would recognize it.

You don't need it, her little voice chimed in. *You've got to be tough to stand on your own.*

"As for me," Laura said, "I am going to slip into my bathing suit, find a nice secluded deck chair to flop into and bury myself in my new book."

Kathi groaned. "Now Laura, I thought we agreed we were going to have fun this week."

"I will be having fun. I like to read."

"You know exactly what I mean." Kathi continued with a mischievous gleam in her blue eyes, "Who knows, there might even be someone on board who can thaw out your heart of ice." One look at the stricken expression on Laura's face told Kathi she'd gone too far. "Oh, Laura, I'm sorry. You know I didn't mean anything by that."

Laura managed a weak smile, but Kathi could see she'd hurt her best friend.

Kathi hugged her tightly, her voice now pleading, "I don't know a kinder, more wonderful person than you." Her blue eyes sought out Laura's dark ones. "I was just teasing you because you're so, well, so independent. You don't need anyone. I admire that in you. Will you please forgive me?"

"You know I forgive you, silly," Laura replied, determined not to expose that tender nerve again. "It's true though, about my heart, I mean. Did you know they called me the 'Ice Princess' at school?"

Of course she knew, Laura thought with dismal certainty. *Everyone knew.* Absently, she twisted the bracelet at her wrist.

"I also know," Kathi was quick to defend, "you were unfairly labeled that way when you refused the advances of that obnoxious frat boy. I would never have believed how far he'd go to spite you. He was vicious."

"It didn't really matter." Laura lied. "My school work kept me busy enough without having to worry about dating." It was true she hadn't had to worry about dating. After that fateful night in her sophomore year, when she'd given in to pressures to accept a date with the most popular boy on campus, she hadn't received more than a handful of invitations. All of which she'd flatly refused.

Looking back to that evening, Laura was still puzzled at how it had all turned out so wrong.

She'd been watching her friends and sorority sisters dating, and it had seemed to Laura at the time that perhaps by entering into a social life, she'd find some happiness and acceptance. She had known there were risks involved. What if she actually fell in love? Her inner voice had screamed she shouldn't chance it, but she silenced the voice and accepted the date.

What she hadn't known was that several of her sorority sisters had engineered the whole thing as a joke. Laura had a reputation of being shy and unreachable, and that rankled them. They thought it hilarious to fix her up with the most sought-after boy on campus; one whose reputation ran to drinking and deflowering young women. He even boasted there wasn't a girl alive that could withstand his charms. All he knew about Laura was that she was lovely and he desired to add her to his list of conquests.

Unaware that she'd been thrown to the lions, Laura went eagerly to the party with him. Within an hour, he was drunk and pawing madly at Laura, making a spectacle of them both before an enthusiastic audience.

After failing numerous attempts to disentangle herself gracefully from his unwanted attentions, Laura angrily slapped his face and marched from the fraternity house with her head held high. No one saw the tears of humiliation that coursed down her cheeks as she fled alone to the comfort of her dormitory.

Being publicly embarrassed was more than his ego could withstand. Within a week, the frat boy had circulated vicious rumors about Laura throughout the small, close-knit campus, effectively cutting off her social life completely.

Rather than admit to their part in the disaster, her sorority sisters perpetuated the cruel rumors. When Laura could stand their contempt no longer, she resigned from the sorority. Ever loyal, Kathi quit the same day.

Interestingly enough, Laura held no malice for them. It was, she believed, her own fault for allowing her guard to drop. She had placed herself in a vulnerable position, and consequently paid the price. It solidified in her mind the need to remain isolated. And confirmed that she was definitely not interested in any entanglements of the heart.

Unaware of the memories stirring within her friend, Kathi chirped, "Hey, I almost forgot. Where's our chaperone? Can I hope since we didn't bring her, that your Dad came to his senses and is letting us go alone?"

Laura was relieved to change the subject. "No such luck. We

have a chaperone all right, although I haven't any idea where he is right now."

"He? Did you say he? You mean to tell me our chaperone is a man?" Kathi sounded incredulous.

"The term man seems a bit optimistic. Try nerd."

Kathi looked stunned. "Okay, I am totally confused. Start from the beginning."

Laura complied with a small groan of displeasure. "It seems Dad has become friends with this guy I knew from high school. He was a neighbor. Graham Kirkland."

She looked at Kathi to see if there was a spark of recognition there, but she found none. Graham would not have been to Kathi's taste, even in high school, Laura thought, and she probably had never even noticed him. "He's a couple of years older than us," she continued, "and a real loser. Tall, gangly, braces, the works. The few times that I was around him, he didn't utter one intelligent word. Graham is an idiot."

"An idiot," Kathi repeated mindlessly. "And just how are we supposed to meet fabulous guys if we have a nerd hanging around?"

"I honestly don't know." Laura picked up the diet cola the stewardess delivered and sipped it thoughtfully. She was wondering if somehow this religion thing had addled her father's brain.

Both girls were silent for a moment. "I've got it!" Kathi exploded, gesturing wildly with her arms. Unfortunately, it was at that moment Laura chose to raise her glass to her lips and Kathi's flailing arms bumped the glass, emptying the contents down the front of Laura's white silk blouse.

"Oh, I'm sorry." Kathi apologized. She grabbed her napkin and tried to help dab up the spill. "I'm so clumsy. I hope I haven't ruined your blouse."

"Not at all." Laura dismissed her help with a wave of her hand. "They'll have a cleaners on board. I'm certain they can get it out. But what was it you were going to tell me?"

"I've got it! The solution to our problem."

Laura was all ears.

"We'll push him overboard!"

"Terrific," Laura replied sarcastically. For one absurd moment she had hoped Kathi did have an idea on how to escape the coming fiasco.

"Now hear me out." Kathi was smiling, making it difficult to tell if she was serious or not. "We'll lure him to the railing by pretending to see something, you know, like a whale or a submarine or something, and when he gets to the edge. . .Wham! Splash! No more Graham."

"I don't know, seems awfully permanent, don't you think?" Laura played along with Kathi's game.

"Well, yes, I suppose it is." Kathi paused for a moment. "How about this? We fix him up with a nerd girl on the ship. That would keep him out of our way." Sudden doubt clouded her blue eyes, and she looked at Laura for confirmation. "He does like girls, doesn't he?"

"Hard to say."

"Hmmm, that could make it difficult." Kathi pursed her lips in deep thought. "I've got it!" She snapped her fingers. She leaned over to grab her carry-on bag that was wedged under the seat. After rummaging noisily through the overstuffed bag for several seconds, she sat up triumphantly, holding a small atomizer in her hands.

"And what, may I ask, is that?" Laura suppressed a chuckle at her friend's antics.

"This, little lady," she whispered conspiratorially, "is the answer to our dilemma." She glanced from side to side, as if to detect possible eavesdroppers. "Top secret formula." She leaned closer to Laura. "Chaperone repellent. One spritz guaranteed to send 'em packin'." She sprayed several short squirts to demonstrate.

Laura sniffed deeply. "Ummmm, smells great, too. How clever of them to disguise it with the scent of Giorgio." She laughed aloud, and Kathi joined in.

"Now, seriously," Laura said, "the way I see it, our best hope is that he misses the ship. Dad never mentioned Graham's flight arrangements, but I assume since he isn't with us that he had to take a later flight. Who knows," she added hopefully, "maybe his flight will be delayed and he'll arrive at the dock to see us sailing off." That comforting thought brought a smile to her face.

"And if he gets aboard before we sail?"

Laura straightened her shoulders in resolve. "Then I'll set him straight from the beginning. I'll explain, kindly, of course, that we don't want or need a chaperone, and he should spend the week pursuing his own interests. I will assure him that my father need not find out."

Laura lowered her voice to an embarrassed whisper, "There is something else, Kathi, something I wasn't going to mention." She could feel her friend's gaze upon her, but she refused to meet it. "It's about Dad and Graham. They're in a Bible study together."

"A Bible study? Do you mean to tell me Howard's got religion?" Kathi was incredulous.

"Yes, uh, well, I'm not actually sure, but I guess so. When he told me, I was so shocked I didn't let him finish." Laura's face flushed at the memory of her angry tirade with her father. "You know, as long as I've known Dad, we've never talked about God before. He didn't even talk about God with Mom, and you remember how religious she was. I don't understand his sudden interest in it. It worries me."

"Listen, Laura," Kathi patted Laura's arm comfortingly. "It's nothing to worry about. People get religious as they get older, all part of the aging process, I think. You know, like losing your hair and stuff. Perfectly normal." She nodded sagely, her dark curls bobbing.

Laura looked somewhat reassured. "I wouldn't have brought it up except that it means Graham must also be, uh, well, religious."

"Like a holy roller?"

"I don't know for sure. I just think we would be wise to expect the worst." Visions of a gangly young man thumping an enormous black Bible swam before Laura. "I wonder if he carries his Bible around with him, like to dinner and stuff. Can you imagine how embarrassing that could be?"

Kathi considered her troubled friend. "Forget about him. We are going to have a great time. . .no matter what."

Graham shifted uncomfortably, trying to find that elusive position in which his legs would fit within the confines of his seat. Even in first class, he felt cramped, as though his knees hovered within inches of his nose. He was delighted no one was seated beside him so he could sit diagonally and stretch his long legs in front of the seat to his left.

Beside him on the vacant seat lay open an enormous black book, dog-eared pages protruding at irregular intervals. He had his tray table down before him as a makeshift desk, and it was buried under a landslide of papers. He sat, bent over the papers, brows furrowed slightly, and after referring to the black book, made several notes.

"Mr. Kirkland, is there something I can do for you?"

Graham considered the attractive stewardess leaning over him for the third time in the last half hour. *Leaving me alone would be nice for starters,* he thought. Aloud he said, "Nothing, thanks."

"Are you sure?" She flashed him a smile.

"Quite." He smiled and returned his attention to his notes, hoping she'd recognize dismissal when she saw it.

Fortunately, at that moment the woman across the aisle called to the stewardess to refresh her drink, and she hurried to comply.

Graham felt a momentary twinge of guilt. He certainly had nothing to be irritable about. True, he disliked flying, but it was just a minor inconvenience. He was here on a mission of mercy.

Graham smiled broadly to himself as he recalled the day he'd vowed to God that he would go anywhere God asked of him to spread the message of salvation. At eighteen years of age, that promise conjured up visions of ministering to impoverished people in remotest China or the wilds of Africa.

It was a heartfelt vow. Graham was so overcome with gratitude for God's saving grace that he wanted to serve Him in some way. But there had been no call. Until now. Finally, years later, Graham was on his way to the mission field—a luxury cruise liner in the Caribbean. And the target of his ministry was a beautiful blond he had admired all his life. Graham chuckled. *God certainly has a sense of humor.*

four

The stewardess came by to collect their trays as the pilot announced the plane had begun its final descent into the Miami Airport. Laura fidgeted with her bracelet, checking the safety clasp for the umpteenth time. Kathi pulled a mirror from her handbag and began to touch up her lipstick. She glanced at her watch and exclaimed, "We better hurry; the ship sails at two!"

The two young women disembarked from the plane in record time. Laura maneuvered quickly through the confusion of milling passengers, her long legs striding easily across the crowded airport. Kathi had to run to keep up. After a brief delay at the revolving carousel where they collected their mountain of luggage, the girls hailed a cab to the docks.

Laura slid into the battered cab beside Kathi who was already giving instructions to the driver. It was obvious that English was his second language and he was having difficulty understanding Kathi's directions. Laura leaned forward and spoke slowly, "We're going on a Majestic Seas Cruise that sails from Pier Three."

To their relief, he nodded and smiled, exposing a mouthful of decayed teeth. "Got it. Cruise. Pier Three." Without hesitation he slammed his foot on the accelerator and jerked the cab into the steady flow of traffic that raced past them.

There had been no need to worry about time. The driver, obviously a seasoned veteran of Miami traffic, fairly flew down the highway, darting in and out of the cars with hair-raising speed. Both women breathed a sigh of relief as the cab screeched to a stop at a sign that read Pier Three.

The Pier was not a wooden structure as Laura had anticipated, but rather an enormous concrete extension of the highway. The signs pointed clearly to the sector where ships from the Majestic Seas Cruise Line boarded from, and they proceeded by cab toward the designated area.

When the driver stopped again, this time at the ship, Kathi lost no time in jumping from the taxi. Laura remained to settle up with the driver, she and Kathi having decided earlier that Laura would handle the business transactions of the trip, and then she too alighted from the cab.

The pungent salt air assailed her senses, and she drew a deep cleansing breath. A warm breeze cavorted about her, snatching at her skirt and whipping through her hair. Sea gulls soared above her, filling the air with their shrill cries. In a moment's time, freed from the stifling air of the cab, she felt refreshed and renewed.

Laura stood mesmerized at the scene before her. There were people everywhere. Some, obviously tourists, were snapping pictures and saying good-byes. Others, dock hands or ship's crew, Laura guessed, loaded boxes and luggage aboard the waiting ship.

And the ship. Nothing could have prepared Laura for the sight of the magnificent ship, the *SS Scandinavia,* anchored at the dock. It was a massive ship standing high above her, its enormous white hull much larger than anything she had envisioned. Its sheer size alone was awe-inspiring.

Reluctantly, Laura dragged her eyes from the ship and turned to suggest to her companion that they get on board. Kathi was nowhere in sight. Laura was standing alone amidst their wide array of belongings. She had been so wrapped up in the bustling activity surrounding her that she had lost track of her friend.

A familiar laugh drew Laura's attention to her far left where she saw Kathi engaged in an animated conversation with a stranger—a very attractive male stranger. Laura smiled. It certainly didn't take Kathi long to begin her vacation. Laura tried waving to catch Kathi's attention, but her efforts were futile. Kathi was too engrossed with this new potential suitor.

With a backward glance toward their luggage, Laura walked over to join them. He was a handsome young man, mid-twenties most likely, with short blond curly hair. He was dressed in a crisp, white uniform, a heavily starched, short-sleeved shirt with navy epaulets on the shoulders and white slacks to match. He was extremely muscular, with biceps that bulged with every movement, and the fabric of his shirt stretched tautly across his massive chest.

"Kathi?" Laura asked, hating to interrupt, but hating more the idea of leaving their things unattended. "Shouldn't we find out what to do with our luggage?"

Kathi unwillingly tore her adoring gaze away from the man and stepped forward to Laura, grasping her hand. "Laura, I'm glad you're here. I'd like you to meet Jack Martin."

Laura accepted Jack's outstretched hand and shook it briefly. "Hello, Jack, it's nice to meet you."

Jack smiled a broad, white smile, "It's my pleasure."

"Jack is with the crew of the *SS Scandinavia*. He's been kind enough to find a porter to take care of our things and to direct us to that building over there," she paused to smile brightly at Jack and then point her many braceleted wrist to a building beside them, "where they will see that we get aboard. Isn't that right, Jack?" Her blue eyes sparkled as she smiled coyly at him once again.

"That's right." He had difficulty dragging his gaze from hers to meet Laura's. "If you'll sign in over there, they'll set you up with room keys and orientation materials. Then, you're on your way."

"Well," Laura said, gently grabbing Kathi's arm, "what are we waiting for?" She turned to Jack and smiled, "Thanks so much for your help." The gentle pressure she applied to Kathi's arm was not working and Laura found herself half dragging her friend toward the one-story building Jack had indicated.

"Good-bye for now," Kathi called over her shoulder. "See you later, I hope." Jack smiled and waved.

Once out of earshot, Laura whispered with exasperation, "You are an outrageous flirt; do you know that?"

Kathi nodded unrepentantly.

Laura laughed at her honesty. "Well, could you at least wait until we get on the ship?"

"He was so cute, there wasn't a moment to lose."

"For heaven's sakes, Kathi, he works for the cruise line! Let's limit our affections to the passengers, shall we? The brochure said there would be almost two thousand passengers, and I'll bet half of them are men, plenty of choices for you."

Kathi shrugged, unconvinced, but allowed Laura to lead her away into the building.

Inside, both women blinked hard, trying to adjust their eyes to the artificially lighted room after being outside in the bright sunlight. It was an office of sorts. Several long, rectangular tables were set up with cards indicating which passengers, by alphabetical order, they would be handling. Laura deposited Kathi in line with the D's and then joined the W line. Smiling employees of the cruise lines took their tickets, confirmed their reservations and accommodations, and within minutes the girls were processed and directed through a door at the back of the office.

"Welcome aboard, ladies. We look forward to sailing with you this week."

"Why, we're already on the ship." Laura spoke her startled thoughts aloud. It had all been so easy. Where was the gangplank surrounded by waving friends that she'd seen in all the old movies? Wasn't she supposed to be covered with the confetti that was flying through the air, tossed by the excited passengers?

"Yes, ma'am," the young man nodded. "You're in the interior of the ship right now. If you have your map handy, I'll show you where we are." Laura shifted the reams of information she had just received into one arm and held the map in her other hand.

"We're right here." The crewman pointed to the map. "On the Compass Deck. And where are your cabins?"

"The Olympic Deck."

"Fine, that's easy. Take the stairs or elevator," he gestured to the right and left, indicating them on both sides, "up to your deck and drop off your things and then report back to the fitness area where they are holding emergency evacuation orientation." He smiled at the puzzled look on Laura's face. "It's a bit overwhelming I know, but I guarantee within two hours, you'll know this place like the back of your hand."

Laura smiled. Knowing her luck with directions, even armed with a map she could be hopelessly lost in a matter of minutes.

She moved aside to let other passengers past. A quick glance at the map indicated they needed to go up six floors. In the interest of time and self-preservation, Laura opted to take the elevator. "This way, Kathi."

Kathi had paid no attention whatsoever to the exchange between Laura and the crewman; instead, she was craning her neck, as if looking for something. "He's gone," she wailed dismally, standing directly in the path of the boarding passengers.

Laura caught Kathi's hand with her free hand and pulled her out of the way. "Who's gone? What are you talking about?"

"Jack. You know, Jack Martin, the blond hunk from outside."

"Oh, him. I'm sure he'll show up later," Laura was more interested in getting to their cabin and unloading her things than she was searching out bell captains. "We need to move on. Did you hear him say we have to attend evacuation practice?"

"Lead the way," came Kathi's despondent reply.

With map in hand, Laura directed them through the ship. Her first impression of the interior of the ship was that it was very similar to a hotel. The long halls were covered in a lush, patterned carpet and the walls were elegantly papered. Pretty lamps were mounted at regular intervals to provide extra lighting in addition to the fluorescent lights suspended overhead.

The crewman had been right; finding the room was fairly easy. Even with the extra time it took for the girls to backtrack once they'd realized Laura was holding the map upside down, they arrived at their room in less than ten minutes. Laura unlocked the door and swung it open.

"Not much to it, is there?" Kathi complained after peeking inside.

Laura followed her in, her gaze sweeping the cabin. It was a fairly small room by hotel standards and simply decorated in comforting neutrals.

Two twin beds constituted the majority of the furnishings. There was a small nightstand between the beds with a reading lamp and telephone, a television mounted on the wall, and a grouping of two upholstered chairs and a table between them, under the window. There was a desk built into the corner, and a huge lighted mirror hanging over it.

"Well, it is rather small," Laura agreed, "but it's kinda nice, don't you think?" She stepped forward to lay her armload of belongings on the bed. "Cozy actually."

"Look, our luggage is already here." Kathi pointed to the row of suitcases standing in front of the mirrored closet doors. She clasped her hands over her heart. "Isn't Jack just *sooo* wonderful? Laura, I can tell already, this is going to be a great week."

Laura smiled indulgently, wishing she held that same conviction. For a brief moment, tears burned at the back of her eyes as she recalled the big plans she had made for this trip, plans now ruined. She couldn't shake the sinking feeling that those plans would affect the rest of her life.

Suddenly, she felt tired, a weariness penetrating down to her bones. Whether it was exhaustion from the traveling or the disappointment of not being able to unburden her tortured mind with her father this week, she wasn't sure, but she sank down into the welcoming softness of the bed and closed her eyes.

five

"Laura? Laura, honey, wake up."

Laura awakened groggy, unable to determine where she was. As she peeked through half-open eyes into the bright blue eyes of Kathi, her memory flooded back. She was on the *SS Scandinavia,* beginning the big vacation she'd been planning for months. But what was she doing lying down?

Laura sat up with a start. "Mercy! I must have fallen asleep." She brushed a strand of golden hair from her eyes. "What time is it?" She glanced sleepily at her watch. "Kathi, it's already three o'clock! We were supposed to meet Graham at three." She jumped off the bed, grabbed her purse and map in one swift motion, and was at the door. "Hurry, we're late."

Kathi smiled sweetly. "I know it, but it's only Graham. He'll wait. You looked so peaceful, I just hated to disturb you."

Laura hugged her. "Thanks for looking after me." A new thought dawned on her, and she groaned, "I've made us miss the evacuation drill too. I'm truly sorry."

"What's to be sorry for? The way I see it, if the ship goes down, we paddle like crazy until someone shows up to save us." Kathi shrugged. "We didn't need a class to tell us that."

Laura laughed at her friend's oversimplification and vowed silently to study up on lifeboats and emergency procedures before bed that night. With her luck, they'd go down like rocks, and while her own life held very little promise, she certainly didn't want to drag her precious friend with her.

With the help of the map Laura clutched in her hand, the girls found their way back to the elevator and down one deck to the International Deck where they were to rendezvous with Graham at the Purser's office.

When Laura and her father had discussed the meeting the night before, it had all seemed so simple, but one look at the sea of passengers crowding into the Purser's office indicated that locating Graham here would be a challenge akin to finding a needle in a haystack.

"Oh great," Kathi moaned. "We'll never find him here. Do we even know what he looks like?"

"No, not exactly." Laura twisted her bracelet. "I didn't expect to have to look through this many people." She paused to assess the situation. "We'll split up. I'll take this side of the room," she motioned to the right, "and you take that side. Look for a tall nerd with dark hair."

"Sure," Kathi giggled. "We'll just go up to all the creeps in the crowd and say 'Hi, I'm looking for my chaperone, and you fit the description of nerd. Could you possibly be Graham Kirkland?'"

"I hadn't even thought about what we'd say to him once we'd found him. What a mess." Laura shook her head in growing aggravation. This all seemed so unnecessary, wasting time looking for someone they wanted to avoid. Why couldn't her father have listened to reason and allowed them to go alone? "Just be tactful, that's all I ask, for my Dad's sake."

She turned to enter the fray, then called back to Kathi whose petite form was already being swallowed up by the crowd, "Whoever finds him first, grab him, and flag down the other."

Kathi nodded and disappeared into the confusion.

Laura considered beginning her search by checking at the Purser's desk for any messages from Graham, when she looked up and found him. Well, she supposed it was him. The man was tall and thin, with dark greasy hair, and he seemed to be looking for someone. *So far,* she thought, *he met all the requirements.*

Their eyes met across the crowded room and when she smiled hesitantly, still unsure that he looked even vaguely familiar, he returned her smile. Assuming his smile to be one of confirmation, she plunged headlong into the crowd to retrieve him.

He's worse than I thought, she shuddered. *And we're stuck with him for an entire week.* Pushing him overboard sounded better all the time.

When Laura looked up from the middle of the room, trying to recapture her bearings, she saw him leaving with a young woman on his arm. She caught a glimpse of a wedding band on his left hand as he opened the door for his companion. Laura sighed audibly, relief written plainly across her face. It wasn't him. The greasy fellow was someone else's problem. *That was a close call.*

Confidence restored, she surveyed the crowd once more. *Too blond. Too attractive. Too married.* Laura mentally checked each of the men before her off her list. A glimmer of hope grew within her. Perhaps Graham had been detained after all. The beginnings of a smile had formed on her lips when, suddenly, her gaze locked with another man standing toward the back of the room.

He was tall, in his mid-twenties, she guessed, and he appeared to be alone. With his dark hair and sharp, gawky features, she knew this had to be him. Heavy-hearted with defeat, she began to press through the thinning crowd toward him when she felt a light touch on her shoulder. Laura glanced back quickly, catching a glimpse of bright yellow. "Good, Kathi, you're here." She continued to move forward toward the man as she spoke, "I've found our man."

Kathi laughed brightly, obviously amused, and this time Laura turned around fully to acknowledge her friend. It was then she noticed Kathi was not alone. She had her arm linked possessively through the arm of a man that personified the phrase, "tall, dark, and handsome."

He was at least 6'4", with dark, wavy hair that curled carelessly at the base of his neck. He had strong, finely chiseled features and a blinding white smile. His handsome face, combined with a golden tan and muscular build, was breathtaking. This man was gorgeous.

The sharp contrast between this man and the gawky one awaiting Laura across the room was painfully evident, and she found herself growing resentful. Not that she had expected anything different. She had known Graham was a nerd. But enough was enough. Here was Kathi clinging to her handsome prince, her second one in less than two hours, while Laura selflessly sought out her toad. Self-pity flooded her.

"I see you've found a suitable companion," Laura snapped, "but haven't you forgotten something?" Without waiting for Kathi's response and rudely ignoring her smiling escort, Laura continued angrily, lowering her voice to a whispered snarl, "we are here to find Graham."

"But Laura," Kathi's laughter rang out, "I have found Graham." She smiled up at the handsome man standing at her side. "Graham Kirkland, I'd like you to meet Laura Wells."

Laura froze, stunned. Silent. *This beautiful man is Graham Kirkland? Impossible.* Even as her mind tried to discount the truth of Kathi's words, Laura felt a crimson flush creep from the soles of her feet to the top of her head.

Graham extended his hand to her in introduction, but Laura's own arm refused to respond. It hung there, rebellious, frozen at her side. *This beautiful man is Graham Kirkland?* Laura's mind repeated dully. *This is Graham Kirkland, the nerd?* She was conscious of the fact that her mouth gaped open slightly, but it, too, seemed frozen.

The sound of Graham's soft chuckle, a deep pleasant sound, roused Laura from her listlessness. "I'm sorry," she mumbled, unable to meet his gaze, "I. . .I didn't expect, I mean I didn't recognize. . ." Laura paused, wishing the ship would indeed sink, at that very moment, and that she would be swallowed up by the sea.

Graham spoke softly to Laura, "Must be the lack of braces that threw you off. I wore them so long people assumed they were a permanent fixture. And, it has been a long time."

Laura heard the gentleness of his voice. Summoning all her courage, she looked up into his eyes. Instead of the mockery she expected to find there, she saw kindness reflected in their depths.

His eyes were gray, a dark, metallic gray, with tiny lines in the corners that indicated he laughed a lot. He was smiling now, and Laura thought they sparkled with glints of blue. He had long, thick lashes, and a penetrating gaze that seemed to see right through her. "It has been a long time," she repeated, unable to look away.

"It must have been, from the description Laura gave me," Kathi bubbled on, unaware of Laura's discomfort. "She had me looking for some sort of ner. . ."

Laura shot her a quelling look before Kathi could relate the unflattering description she had been given. Laura flushed again, when she peeked over at Graham and realized he knew exactly what they had been expecting.

Graham smiled broadly, apparently amused with the whole situation, exposing a mouthful of perfect, dazzling white teeth. Laura swallowed hard, her heart pounding in her chest. *Well,* she thought wryly, remembering her earlier conversation with her father where she had vehemently proclaimed it would take a miracle to make Graham even passable, *I am looking at a walking miracle.*

"It's great to finally see you both, I've been looking forward to this meeting," Graham magnanimously changed the subject. Conscious of the fact that the noise of the crowd made it difficult to communicate without shouting, he suggested, "Maybe it would be easier to talk if we went outside." He slipped a well-muscled arm around the back of each girl and guided them out of the office into the hall just outside.

Standing in the relative quiet of the corridor, beside Graham, the unexpected epitome of perfect manhood, Laura belatedly considered her own appearance. With their rush to meet him, she hadn't even sought out a mirror to see how she looked.

A downward glance confirmed her fears. Her once crisp, navy linen suit was now hopelessly wrinkled, testimony to the fact that she'd slept in it, and her white blouse wore the telltale brown stain from her earlier mishap with the Diet cola.

A self-conscious hand stole up to inspect her chignon and once again her worst fears were realized. Even without a mirror, she knew by the abundance of escaped hair that the elegant coiffure she had worn that morning had deteriorated into a tangled mess that now hung limply around her shoulders.

To make matters worse, she could feel Graham's eyes upon her as he too studied her appearance, and she knew he must be comparing it to Kathi who looked fresh and well rested in her chic, canary-yellow outfit.

Laura flushed hotly again. She twisted the bracelet at her wrist in embarrassed agitation. The combined humiliation of the way she had behaved with the way she looked was mortifying. *I can't wait for the off chance that the ship will sink,* she thought. *That could prolong this agony indefinitely. My only hope is to dash to the nearest exit and throw myself headlong into the sea.*

Again, Graham came to her rescue. "It's been a long day," he said. "Suppose I escort you two back to your room to unpack and rest. I can pick you up before dinner, and we can get to know each other better then."

Laura's downcast face lit up at the unexpected reprieve. "Would you mind terribly?" Her heart nearly burst with gratitude for his undeserved compassion. She offered a shy smile of appreciation. "That would be wonderful."

"But we haven't seen anything of the ship yet!" Kathi complained, obviously reluctant to let Graham out of her sight. "I wanted to take a tour."

Graham flashed her his dazzling smile. "Suppose I pick you up an hour early. That will give you time to relax, and we'll still have time for a thorough tour before dinner."

Any argument that Kathi had melted at the sight of his smile. "It's a terrific idea," she cooed, batting her blue eyes coyly. "How thoughtful you are."

"Oh, I almost forgot." Graham stepped over to one of the groupings of tables and chairs that were scattered throughout the hall. "I'd hate to leave these behind." Laying on top of the table was an enormous, well-worn, black book, with an open notebook full of scrawled notes beside it. He reached over to scoop them up.

Laura and Kathi exchanged knowing glances. The surprise of his good looks and pleasant personality had temporarily distracted them from the fact that their chaperone was a religious nerd. Here was proof: he drags his huge Bible with him everywhere.

Laura rolled her eyes behind his back, acknowledging that she had been duped. Kathi began to giggle. The notion of a handsome holy roller was just too funny. The giggles were infectious and Laura found herself unwillingly succumbing.

Graham stood up, books grasped under his arm, and considered the laughing pair standing before him. With one eyebrow raised in question he asked, "What's so funny? Have I missed something?" His gray eyes searched their faces for clues.

"It's your Bible. . ." Kathi laughed.

"My Bible?" Graham held out the black book. "This? It's not a Bible. It's a directory of sporting goods retailers in the United States. My family owns a sporting goods wholesaling business, and I promised my father I'd research some potential customers if I had any free time. What made you think it was my Bible?" His look was genuinely puzzled.

"We know you are real religious. . ." Kathi began.

"Dad said you were in a Bible study together, and Kathi and I assumed that you'd. . ." Laura's attempt at an explanation drifted off into embarrassed silence as she realized she had misjudged him again and had probably insulted him deeply. She wondered if it was too late to heave herself overboard. Her eyes lowered guiltily to the floor, and she fidgeted nervously with her bracelet.

To the amazement of both women, Graham began to laugh. A truly hearty laugh. A deep resonant sound that brought sweet shivers down Laura's spine. His gray eyes sparkled with mirth as he said, "I can tell I have a formidable reputation with you two. It's a wonder you didn't have me thrown overboard when I arrived."

"We thought about it," Kathi answered solemnly, nodding her head in affirmation.

Graham threw back his head and roared laughter. This time the girls joined in, Laura somewhat hesitantly, as the humor of the situation along with the relief that Graham wasn't offended struck home.

They were still laughing as Graham deposited them at their cabin. "I'll be back for you at seven."

❧

Graham closed the door to his cabin and rested his tall frame against it. Leaning his head back on the polished wood, he closed his eyes and sighed heavily.

"Father, I'm having second thoughts about our arrangement. It's not that I don't want to do it, You understand, it's just that I feel so inadequate." Graham paused for a moment, and the memory of soft, brown eyes framed with feathery lashes filled his mind. Deep within the depths of those mahogany pools was reflected a vulnerability and pain he hadn't expected.

"She's different than I expected, Lord. She's not the self-sufficient young woman I always thought her to be." He hadn't actually known Laura in school, he had been much older and not the sort that attracted much female attention. But he had known of her, and like all the other guys at school, he had admired her. She had been so beautiful and so poised. He had imagined she had all the confidence he lacked.

"There's a hurt there, one I know You want to heal. But she thinks I'm the enemy. How can I help if I can't get close?" Graham fell silent and a familiar scripture came to his mind. "Not by might, not by power, but by my Spirit, says the Lord." Graham grinned as he raised his eyes toward heaven, "Thanks for the reminder. Forgive me for my faithlessness. I'm back on the case."

six

"What time is it now?" Kathi called from the desk which had been transformed into a dressing table. She was artfully applying the finishing touch to her cosmetics from the multitude of pots and containers surrounding her.

"It's two minutes later than the last time you asked me," Laura replied with amused exasperation. "He should be here in less than five minutes."

That pronouncement spurred Kathi on to a new flurry of excited activity. One last glance of approval at her image in the lighted mirror, and she jumped up to spin around before Laura. "How do I look?" Her blue eyes searched Laura's face anxiously, seeking reassurance.

"You look lovely, as always, and I feel certain you'll dazzle him as you have all your past suitors," Laura answered honestly, her brown eyes smiling warmly at her friend.

Kathi's dress, a strapless confection with a short tiered skirt, complimented her curvaceous frame perfectly, and its vivid blue color was a perfect match for her eyes. Sparkling earrings, a cascade of rhinestones, dangled from her earlobes, and a glittering rhinestone necklace completed the ensemble. Kathi had taken no chances tonight, Laura noted; she had dressed with the obvious intent of overwhelming Graham. And Laura knew she would succeed.

Strangely enough, Laura, too, felt a burgeoning sense of anticipation as the hour that Graham was to return approached. *Not for the same reason, of course,* she reassured herself, and her frantic little voice that had been screaming dire warnings at her all afternoon. *Stay away from Graham,* it ordered. *Keep your distance from him. He can only bring trouble and heartache.*

He doesn't pose a threat, she responded confidently to the

43

nagging little voice. No, she wasn't interested in him. She wasn't interested in anyone. She was a loner.

And even if she weren't a loner, she reasoned further, she wouldn't be interested in Graham. After all, they were complete opposites. He was everything she wasn't, especially the religious part. Definitely not her type, she concluded.

Who cares if he is kind and considerate, not to mention fabulous looking? He is nothing more than an unwelcome replacement for my father on this trip.

Well, she amended slightly after giving the matter some thought, *he is hard to dislike. He's been so solicitous, and Kathi thinks he's wonderful, so I guess I like him, just a little, for Kathi's sake.* Graham and Kathi would be perfect for each other; they were both beautiful and confident and joyfully optimistic, a perfect couple. But as far as having Graham to herself, Laura simply wasn't interested.

All the same, Laura had dressed with special care that evening. She had chosen a sleeveless, black chemise of silk shantung that buttoned up the back from the hem to the neckline. It was a favorite of hers, simple and flattering, and it provided her with a look of sophisticated confidence, something she desperately needed after her disastrous first meeting with Graham.

She pulled her thick, straight hair back into an elaborate knot at the nape of her neck and added a single strand of lustrous pearls at her throat to finish the look. The image she saw reflected back in the mirror was one of a self-assured, competent young woman. Laura smiled in approval. Graham would see she was not a blushing idiot after all.

Promptly at seven, there was a sharp knock at the door. Kathi stood immobilized, trying to determine if she would make the best impression by answering the door, and possibly risk looking overanxious, or by having Laura answer the door and risk diluting her dramatic entrance. Laura, sensing her dilemma, opened the door to their guest.

If possible, Laura thought with some annoyance, *Graham looks even more handsome than before.* He was dressed in khaki slacks and a white shirt open at the collar with a navy sports coat. His dark hair curled in soft waves on his forehead, framing his tanned features.

He flashed her his brilliant smile, his gray eyes sparkling appreciatively. "Hello, Laura. You look great!"

It took her a moment to catch her breath. "Hi, Graham," Laura responded casually, hoping he could not hear her heart slamming against her chest. "Kathi is all ready to go. You two have a wonderful tour, and I'll meet you in the dining room at eight." She tried to sound indifferent despite the breathless quality of her voice. What was it about this man that made her act so strangely, she wondered. Maybe she was just hungry.

"You're coming, too, aren't you?" Graham asked, his steely gray eyes locked onto hers.

"No, well, yes," Laura stammered, blushing furiously. "What I mean is, I'll join you for dinner at eight. I thought you and Kathi might enjoy touring alone."

"No, it'll be more fun if we all go together. Right, Kathi?"

Kathi appeared around the door, and smiled weakly, obviously disappointed with the plans. Laura knew Kathi hadn't intended to share Graham with anyone, but she couldn't very well say so graciously, so Laura offered, "I'm not quite ready yet, why don't you two go on without me?"

"If you insist." Kathi was all smiles as she reached for Graham's arm. "We'll see you in the dining room."

"We'll wait." The finality in Graham's tone of voice indicated the decision was made. They were all going together. Laura shot a quick look of apology to Kathi and went inside to get her purse.

Disappointed, but not defeated, Kathi locked her arm through Graham's and began to prattle on animatedly about anything that came to mind. By the time they had reached the elevator at the end of the hall, Laura could see that Graham was thoroughly captivated by her lovely friend.

With Kathi monopolizing the conversation and her own presence forgotten, Laura decided to use the opportunity to study their home for the coming week.

Their whirlwind tour began with a stop on the deck below to an elegant theater furnished with plush velvet seats and ornately gilded walls. Graham explained that they could attend a Broadway musical here, or any of a dozen other live performances.

From there, they took a quick stroll up the International Deck. Laura thought it resembled the shopping mall from home. The wide, flagstone corridor was flanked by quaint shops and stylish boutiques boasting a vast array of wares. Tucked in between the shops were cozy lounges where passengers might stop to rest and take refreshment or simply sit and watch fellow travelers strolling by. There was even an ice cream parlor to satisfy a sweet tooth.

At the sight of food, Laura's stomach growled ferociously, reminding her it had been neglected that day. Laura looked up, embarrassed, hoping Graham and Kathi hadn't heard the rumblings. To her relief, they were so engrossed with one another that she doubted they would have noticed if she had shouted.

Laura knew a momentary twinge of loneliness as she considered her two companions. They had hit it off perfectly as she had known they would, and she told herself she was happy for them. They belonged together. It was just that seeing them together was a painful reminder of the solitude that engulfed her. A once comfortable solitude that now closed in oppressively.

You don't need them, her little voice admonished, *you don't need anyone.*

For a split second, Laura entertained a traitorous thought so revolutionary that she wondered where it came from. *Maybe I do need someone. Maybe I do.*

There was no time to ponder that latest thought because the three of them had reached the end of the International Deck and Graham was pushing open the heavy doors leading outside. The girls stopped suddenly, awestruck by the glittering scene before them. Kathi, temporarily silenced, found her voice and began chattering excitedly, pulling Graham out farther to inspect the deck while Laura hung back mesmerized by the beautiful display.

It was dusk, and to dispel the evening shadows rapidly approaching, the deck was illuminated with hundreds of flickering lights. There were candles atop each table, firelight dancing within the protection of their glass globes, and flaming torches standing sentry at regular intervals to cast their golden, glowing light. Strands of tiny, white lights twinkled festively from the railing. It was like a magical fairy land.

A steady breeze, fragrant with the salty aroma of the sea, buffeted Laura about, jeopardizing her carefully coiled hair and tugging playfully at the hem of her dress. She hardly noticed, so enchanted was she by the spectacle before her.

At the far side of the deck, a group of men clad in native garb played calypso music on steel drums. The lilting tune was a perfect complement to the sparkling lights. There was a lightheartedness here. The music and lights were so joyful, they seemed to beckon her to be a part of it. To relinquish the turmoil of her thoughts and find tranquility. If only she knew how.

"It's nearly eight," Graham's deep voice whispered, his warm breath tickling her ear. "We need to get down to the dining room. Are you ready?"

Laura jumped, startled by his closeness. She had been so involved with her thoughts she hadn't noticed his approach. She was glad for the darkness, hoping it would mask the telltale flush she felt burning on her cheeks. What was it about this man that made her feel this way? Must be a touch of seasickness. "I'm ready."

"Wow! Wasn't that the most beautiful place you've ever been?" Kathi bubbled with enthusiasm. "Graham promised he'd bring us back after dinner; it's so romantic." She flashed an inviting smile at him. Laura vowed silently to make herself scarce after dinner so she wouldn't intrude on their romantic evening.

Several decks below, at the base of a graceful winding staircase, they found the formal dining hall where they would be taking most of their meals. The area immediately outside the dining room was crowded with well-dressed passengers, waiting to be admitted. In the corner, partially concealed by several large green plants, a man in a tuxedo played a grand piano, providing soft, background music for the guests.

Laura smiled in silent approval. If Kathi and she were disappointed with the simplicity of their cabin, the tour had provided them with enough grandeur to make up for what their own quarters lacked. Here was the elegance Laura had imagined she would find on a cruise.

From top to bottom, the ship was outfitted with the finest materials and workmanship. Rich fabrics, gleaming hardwoods, and polished brass were in abundance. Original oil paintings by renowned artists hung on the walls and objets d'art were tastefully displayed throughout the ship.

"Let's eat." Graham steered the women past the crowd, through the double doors into the dining room. They were met by a maitre d', resplendent in a black tuxedo, who, after asking their names and consulting a master list, directed them to their assigned table.

The dining room was, in Laura's estimation, by far the grandest room that they had seen. It was a huge room, with a high, domed ceiling lavishly trimmed with intricately detailed molding. From the highest point hung a magnificent chandelier glittering with thousands of faceted crystals. Recessed lights in the ceiling supplemented the lighting, bestowing a warm glow on the tables and company below.

Their table, located toward the center of the room, was covered with a white linen tablecloth and set with fresh flowers and candles. By the time they arrived, a few minutes past eight, there were three other people already seated, the people that would be their dinner companions for the duration of the week.

Graham stepped forward and introduced himself and the girls to the waiting guests, and the three of them were seated. Laura hung back, pretending to adjust the hem of her skirt, allowing Kathi to select the seat next to Graham before she sat down. Kathi flashed her a quick grin to show her appreciation. Laura took the seat on the end, next to the man introduced as Robert Gleason, and across from Graham.

Robert seemed visibly relieved when they joined the party, and it didn't take Laura long to figure out why. The couple sitting at the other end of the table, Linda and Blaine Johnson, were newlyweds and so enamored with each other, they didn't join in the conversation, other than to give a perfunctory one or two word reply to questions addressed specifically to them. Even then, they would not look up from the tender gaze they leveled on each other. Laura found herself smiling. It was obvious they were so in love that they were not aware of their rude behavior.

Almost immediately, a smartly dressed waiter appeared and placed before each of them a plate of marinated shrimp and crab. The food had been artistically arranged, and Laura hated to disturb it. The others had already begun to eat with gusto, so she joined in. It was delicious, and she savored each bite.

For several minutes a quiet settled over the crowded dining room, as the patrons busied themselves with their food. By the time the main course had arrived and appetites had been somewhat sated, the room was filled once again with the pleasant din of conversation.

Robert initiated the conversation at their table, asking everyone to tell where they were from and what they did. The Johnsons, as expected, never looked up, but Blaine did give a brief reply. "We're from Tulsa, and we're on our honeymoon." He smiled tenderly at his wife.

Kathi giggled and turned to Graham, "Isn't that just so romantic?" Without waiting for a response, she looked across at Robert and proceeded to regale him with a five-minute synopsis of her life, Laura's life, and how they came to be with Graham. She completed her dissertation with, "And even though I haven't known Graham for very long, I can just tell that we are going to be the best of friends." She turned to Graham and gave him her most beguiling smile.

Laura marveled as she watched her vivacious friend. Kathi may not have a clue as to what goes on in the business world or the world at all for that matter, but she was a master when it came to men. Within minutes, she could have them eating out of her hand.

Laura's own inadequacies seemed glaring in comparison. She

could handle men in a business setting with no problem. A business associate did not pose a threat; they could never get close enough to hurt her. Her trademark aloof detachment actually worked to her advantage there. People equated her reserve with competence and sophistication.

But as far as dealing with people socially, especially men, she was truly glad no one could see inside her, past her cool exterior to the insecure mess lurking within.

"What about you, Laura?" Robert asked, thoughtfully trying to draw her into the conversation. "Tell me about you."

All eyes were riveted on Laura and she tugged her bracelet with embarrassment. "There's nothing much to say," she murmured shyly. "I just graduated in accounting, and after the cruise, I'll begin work with a firm back home." She toyed with the food on the plate, hoping her answer had been sufficient to direct attention elsewhere.

"Wow," Robert answered. "I would never have guessed you're an accountant!"

The arched eyebrow that Laura turned to him indicated she had mistaken his meaning.

"Oh, not that you couldn't handle it. It's just such a waste, that's all." Robert lowered his voice and stared into Laura's velvety brown eyes. "You're too beautiful to be an accountant, locked away with ledgers all day. I had you pegged as a model for sure."

Unaccustomed to such bold admiration, Laura did not know how to respond. She self-consciously lowered her eyes and squirmed uncomfortably in her chair, hoping his remark had gone unnoticed. Evidently, it had not. For a split second, Graham's eyes lost their usual merry sparkle and he turned a steely glance at Robert.

"So, Robert," his voice was cool, "you haven't told us anything about yourself."

Laura again found herself indebted to Graham for delivering her from embarrassment. She wondered at the less than congenial tone of voice he used with Robert, but smiled as she realized he had taken his role as chaperone seriously. He was trying to protect her from any unwanted advances. Maybe her Dad had been right to send him.

Robert complied with Graham's request, evidently unaware anything was amiss. "I'm a pilot for a small commercial airline based out of Atlanta." His brown eyes shone with pride. "Our runs are limited to flying within the continental US, and I usually handle the flights on the east coast. I guess that's why I chose a cruise for a vacation, I wanted to see something other than the sky."

Robert's comments about being an airline pilot sparked a lively conversation over dessert and coffee, with even the Johnsons participating, and by the end of the meal, each of the travelers felt a sense of camaraderie with their new-found friends.

It was late by the time the waiter began to clear away the dessert plates, and the Johnsons excused themselves for the evening. As if on cue, the others rose to leave.

"It's been a lovely evening; I hate to see it end so soon." Robert addressed his comment to Laura, who was already composing a plausible excuse for leaving Kathi and Graham to their romantic walk on deck.

"We're going for a walk out on the deck," Kathi interjected, before Laura could escape. "Perhaps you'd like to join us, Robert?" Laura shot her a withering glance.

"Great." He turned a warm smile on Laura.

"I'd like to freshen up a moment first," Kathi said. "Laura, won't you come with me? I just know I'll get lost without you." She stared pointedly at Laura, indicating she wanted to speak to her in private.

Laura turned to the men. "Will you excuse us please?"

They were scarcely inside the ladies' room when Kathi grabbed Laura's hand, her blue eyes pleading. "Laura, I need a big favor from you."

"Sure, what do you need?"

"I need you to flirt with Robert," Kathi stated matter of factly.

"What?" Laura was incredulous. "What are you talking about? You've got to be kidding! No way."

"No, now listen." Kathi drew her to a small couch in the corner of the powder room and perched beside her. "I can't get Graham's full attention with you around. . ."

Laura rolled her eyes in amused tolerance at her friend's characteristic bluntness.

"What I mean is," Kathi amended, "Graham is so conscientious that he doesn't want to do anything unless all three of us are together. I guess he feels as a chaperone he's got to entertain the both of us."

Laura nodded her agreement thus far.

"Three is not exactly a romantic number, if you know what I mean. If Graham knew you were happy with Robert's company, he would feel free to concentrate his attention on me." Kathi looked contrite for a moment. "I guess I sound really selfish, don't I? It's just that Graham is special. . .do you understand what I am trying to say?"

"I understand perfectly, but I can stay out of your way without involving Robert. I'll just go back to the cabin and read."

"No, that won't work." Kathi shook her head. "You've got to be with someone. Graham has got to think you would prefer to be with Robert rather than with us, then he'll be freed of the responsibility of watching over you every minute."

"I'm sorry, Kathi, but I just can't." Visions of her disastrous date with the frat boy loomed over Laura. She couldn't explain her fears to Kathi, the devastation she carried from the last time she had taken a risk on a relationship. "I'm not ready to get involved with anyone." *Now or ever,* she thought to herself.

"I'm not asking you to get involved with him, certainly not in a romantic way. I just want you to make friends with him, so that you two can spend time together." She could see that Laura remained unconvinced. "Laura, I'm not suggesting a commitment of the heart, I just want a little time alone with Graham, to see if there is something between us. It's real important to me." Kathi's eyes were imploring. "All I'm asking you to do is a little harmless flirting."

"I don't know, Kathi. . ." Laura's voice reflected her uncertainty. "Even if I agree to this idiotic scheme, I don't know how to flirt."

Kathi smiled, sensing a forthcoming victory. "It's easy. Just look into his eyes and smile. Act like everything he says is the cleverest thing you've ever heard. Trust me, I saw the way he looked at you. All he needs is the slightest encouragement, and he'll be eating out of your hand."

"I don't know. I've got a bad feeling about this."

"What's the matter? Don't you like Robert?"

"Sure, he seems nice enough, but. . ."

"He's good looking, intelligent, mature, gainfully employed, all the qualities you should look for in a man. What could possibly go wrong?" Kathi questioned gaily.

Lots of things, Laura thought. Aloud she said, "Why do I let you bully me into these things?"

Kathi hugged her tightly, taking her last statement to be one of assent. "Trust me, it'll be fine. What could possibly go wrong?"

seven

This is easy, Laura mused as she stood at the deck railing, watching out over the stern of the ship. She marveled again at the wealth of knowledge Kathi had amassed about men. Just as she had said, all Laura had to do to encourage the friendship between her and Robert was to nod and smile at the appropriate time. *Nothing to it.*

Actually, this confidence she was enjoying was a very recent acquisition. Less than an hour ago, when Robert first suggested that Laura stroll with him on the deck and Kathi took Graham in the opposite direction, Laura's reaction was sheer panic. She didn't want the four of them to be separated, and she certainly didn't want to be alone with Robert.

Panic gave way to nausea, and Laura had to take deep gasping breaths to keep from throwing up. Her hands got so clammy that every few moments she wiped her palms on her dress to dry them. While she was sure that Robert was blissfully unaware of her discomfort, the night was still young.

Suppose she suddenly fainted or became sick. How would she explain that? By casually remarking it was how she reacted to all men? Not hardly. In desperation, Laura sought to revive herself with a mental pep talk. It's only a walk with a friend, no big deal. Certainly not fatal. After chanting "No big deal, certainly not fatal" several times in a whispered monotone, she was able to subdue her nausea, regulate her breathing, and accompany Robert, albeit reluctantly, on the deck.

To see her now, it would be difficult to believe her earlier panic. She was the picture of calm sophistication. Robert stood beside her at the railing and the two of them stared silently into the frothy wake marking their path through the blackened sea. It was a companionable silence broken by the occasional observation

54

that Robert would make.

Laura said little, content to listen to him and the sounds of the night: the gentle hum of the ship's engines, the murmur of the ocean waves breaking against the ship, and the sporadic snatches of music or conversation carried along on the salty breeze.

Laura took the opportunity to surreptitiously study her companion. She guessed he must be in his early thirties. He was attractive in a boyish sort of way, with short, dark hair and serious brown eyes. *Certainly not gorgeous like Graham.*

She pushed the wayward thought away. She didn't want to be thinking about Graham. Graham was Kathi's. They were perfect together. *Anyway, I'm not the least bit interested in him,* she assured herself.

"So, you and Kathi have been friends since the second grade. It must be great to have such a close friend." Robert's voice interrupted her thoughts.

"With Kathi around, life is never dull, that's for sure." Laura laughed.

"She and Graham really seem to be an item, don't they?" His voice was slightly teasing as he continued, "Must be one of those torrid shipboard romances I read about in the brochures. Don't they guarantee one for each passenger?" His eyebrow arched slightly as he turned to face her.

Robert's glance drifted slowly over Laura, and she immediately felt uneasy. Surely, he didn't think she was looking for a shipboard romance. She had only agreed to spend time with him to stay out of Kathi's way. Suddenly, it didn't look like such a fool-proof plan after all.

Pretending to discover something of interest over to her left, she moved a step away, putting as much distance as she could between them without being too obvious. As he stepped toward her, his dark eyes studying her face, Laura's heart lurched within her. The look in his eyes was unmistakably predatory. She would have to say something quickly, before he got the wrong idea.

"There you are!" Graham announced, stepping unexpectedly from the shadows. "Time to turn in for the night." Laura thought he was even more handsome with dark windblown curls framing his face. He smiled at her and spoke with fatherly concern, "You've had a long day, and I don't want Howard to think that I let you wear yourself out." He smiled briefly toward her escort as he reached out to take Laura's arm and direct her toward the door. "See you tomorrow, Robert."

Laura couldn't believe her good fortune. *What timing.* Graham seemed to have a real knack for pulling her out of tight places. Belatedly, she remembered her manners. "Goodnight, Robert," Laura called over her shoulder as she was being led away. "See you tomorrow."

"I'll walk you to your cabin," he offered, as he fell in step with them, "since I'll probably turn in myself." He sounded somewhat disgruntled.

Kathi was waiting for them in the hall, a pretty pout on her lips. The four of them proceeded to the girls' cabin in silence. Laura had the distinct impression that both Kathi and Robert were unhappy with the way the evening was concluding.

As for Laura, she couldn't be happier. She'd given her friend time alone with her current beau and managed to get away without incident. She practically skipped to their room, humming a tune she had heard performed earlier that evening by the calypso band.

Upon arrival at the cabin, an unwelcome thought dampened her enthusiasm like a shower of ice-cold water. Suppose Robert wanted to kiss her good night. She knew that was a fairly common practice, but she wanted no part of it. Just considering the possibility made her palms grow clammy. Silently, she berated Kathi. *How could I have let her talk me into this charade.*

Fortunately, her fears went unrealized. Graham stood at the door, looking every bit like an overprotective father, and watched Robert expectantly. Robert, either because of his gentlemanly upbringing or because of the ferocious gray stare Graham had leveled on him, bade them all a good night and, with a quick smile to Laura, was gone.

Laura released her breath in a long sigh. She had been so nervous, she'd forgotten to exhale. She had survived the night. Kathi was right; there had been nothing to worry about. She smiled brightly at Kathi and Graham and slipped into the cabin, allowing them a moment of privacy to say good night.

Kathi entered the cabin minutes later, her pretty face flushed, and Laura braced herself for a full report of her evening. To Laura's amazement, none came. It wasn't until much later, after the girls were settled into their beds for the evening that Kathi spoke at all.

"You know, Laura, Graham's not like other guys." Kathi's wistful voice penetrated the darkness of the cabin.

"Well, if anybody would know that, it would be you. You're the uncontested expert on men," Laura teased.

"I'm serious, Laura, he's, he's . . .different. I've never met anyone like him. I suppose it's because he's religious."

"I'm not sure I understand."

"Take tonight, for instance. After we left you and Robert, I led Graham out to a deserted part of the deck. There I was, smelling like an angel in my Passion perfume, which is guaranteed to make the men go crazy, dressed in my knock 'em dead, strapless blue dress, standing beside the most fabulous-looking guy I've ever seen.

"We stood there, side by side, silently watching the stars. It was as though we were the only two people on the whole earth." Kathi's voice drifted off to barely a whisper. Then suddenly, to emphasize her words, she sat bolt upright in the bed and stared at Laura through the shadows. The travel clock dial cast a greenish glow over her features. "I'm telling you, it was so romantic, I got goose bumps."

Laura fought the urge to laugh at her friend and point out that it usually took a half-price sale on shoes to warrant goose bumps. She decided against it. She didn't want to hurt her feelings by making light of this current infatuation.

"Anyway, I looked up into his eyes, which are incredible by the way, and I whispered in my sexiest voice, 'What are you thinking about?'" Kathi sat forward, perched on the edge of the bed. "Do you know what he answered?"

Laura shook her head, afraid to hear.

"He said, 'I was just thinking about what an amazing God we serve. He's the all-powerful Creator of the universe, the sea, and the stars, and yet He's intimately concerned about each one of us. I find such comfort in that.'" Kathi's voice dropped off. "Laura, my mouth hung open like a codfish, just like yours did this afternoon when you met Graham."

Laura winced at the unpleasant memory.

"From all indications," Kathi continued, somewhat incredulously, "it looks like he found my irresistible charms resistable. I just don't understand it." She shook her head, genuinely puzzled. "The only way I can figure it is that maybe he was a nerd so long that he's real new to this romantic business, and I'll have to break him in slowly. Anyway, if you and Robert can disappear for a while tomorrow, I'll try out a new approach."

Laura's heart sank. "Me and Robert?" She gulped. She was so confident that tonight had been her first and last outing with him.

"Oh, Laura, I wouldn't ask you to do it if it weren't so important to me." Kathi moved across the room and sat on the edge of Laura's bed. "I think Graham might be the one. He just needs a little more coaxing to realize it." She took Laura's hand into her own. "You do like Robert, don't you? I mean you had fun with him tonight, didn't you?"

Laura was silent for a moment as she considered her options. If she said she had fun with Robert, then she would most assuredly have to be his companion tomorrow. Her palms began to sweat at the thought.

On the other hand, if she told Kathi the truth, that she wasn't the least bit interested in Robert and would prefer to spend the day reading her new novel, then Kathi would not ask her to accompany Robert, but Kathi would not have the opportunity to pursue Graham without distraction.

The decision was easily made. If Kathi thought Graham was "the one," then Laura could do her part by entertaining Robert for another day or two. It was a small price to pay for her best friend's happiness. "Yes, we had fun and yes, I do like Robert." Laura tried to make her voice reflect enthusiasm she didn't feel.

Kathi threw her arms around Laura and hugged her tightly. "Do you mean it?" Without waiting for a response she rattled on excitedly. "You know, I thought there might be something between you two when I saw that big smile on your face after he left tonight. I do believe you were even humming a love song." She drew back to look directly into Laura's face. "Can you believe that this is happening? I mean, we've both found special men, right here on the ship. It's so romantic. You know, I always dreamed it would be like this. Maybe we can even have a double wedding."

Laura's eyes widened in horror, and she started to speak, to correct her friend's gross misperception about the depth of her feelings for Robert, but Kathi interrupted, oblivious to Laura's plight. "This is so great." She flounced back over to her own bed and scrambled under the covers. "This is so great," she repeated gaily as she patted the blanket over her. "Did you ever imagine anything like this happening, even in your wildest dreams?"

No, never, Laura thought glumly, falling back against her pillow. *I couldn't have imagined this big of a mess if I had tried.* She wrestled briefly with the idea of explaining to Kathi exactly how she felt about Robert, but she knew it was no use. Kathi had her mind made up.

Laura sought comfort in the fact that it was a harmless deception, and that she was actually helping her friend achieve happiness. And it wasn't a lie, exactly. She liked Robert, sort of. Not as much as she liked Graham.

Laura sat up with a jolt. For the second time that evening, she was troubled with unwanted thoughts about Graham. *Graham was Kathi's, for heaven's sake,* she told herself. *And anyway,* she reassured herself, *I'm not interested in him. Not in the least.*

Within minutes, Laura could hear the steady breathing of her roommate, indicating Kathi had found peaceful slumber. Her own jumbled thoughts would allow her no rest.

In spite of the companionship she now found herself inundated with, much of it unwelcome, deep loneliness still blanketed her, its sharp talons gripping her unmercifully. She grasped at a fleeting thought, and for a second, the tiny spark of hope that flickered tenuously within her breast burned brightly, as she remembered her father and the plan she would present him when she got home. Maybe he could help after all.

Her little voice, uncharacteristically quiet for the evening, chose this moment to unload on her. *Don't you understand?* it screeched, *There is no help. You can't trust anyone. You've got to make it alone. People will hurt you.* Fledgling hope was extinguished. The black void inside her seemed to expand, making it difficult to breathe. She lay motionless on her bed, tears of desolation stinging her eyes.

For Laura, the wait for sleep was long, and her dreams were hardly peaceful.

eight

Laura rolled over, trying to focus her sleep-heavy eyes on the travel clock beside her. *Six o'clock.* Summoning all her will power, she dragged her reluctant body from the comfortable bed and silently made her way to the bathroom, careful not to disturb Kathi who slept peacefully.

Within minutes Laura reappeared, somewhat more alert after scrubbing her face in ice-cold water. She was dressed in her customary running attire, navy shorts, a plain white t-shirt, and her slightly scuffed tennis shoes. Her thick, golden hair was restrained in a single braid that hung past her shoulders.

She glanced over at her sleeping roommate and smiled. Kathi was not a morning person and, barring a nuclear explosion, it was unlikely she would rise before noon. Without a sound, Laura slipped through the door and latched it behind her.

A few yards from their cabin door was the door leading outside to the jogging deck. Laura had selected their cabin on the Olympic Deck for that reason. She stepped out into the silvery shadows of early morning. All was quiet now, save for the rhythmic hum of the ship's engines. The ever-present breeze met her with a brisk greeting, carrying with it the welcome salty spray of the sea. She paused to breathe deeply of the cleansing air. In spite of her restless night, Laura felt unexpectedly refreshed.

She performed a few perfunctory stretches, readying her still sluggish limbs for her regular morning workout. Satisfied that she was sufficiently limber, she began to move. She started slowly at first, loping along at a comfortable pace, then, as her long legs warmed to the challenge, she broke into a run.

The polished wood jogging track made a complete circle around the perimeter of the ship. Laura had nearly completed her second pass when she spotted a tall figure up ahead. Until now, with the exception of Laura, the deck had been deserted. She thought the person looked vaguely familiar, with his broad shoulders and dark, wavy hair, but she dismissed the idea as ludicrous. *Why would anybody else be up at this hour?*

Graham stood up from his stretching at her approach, a lazy smile spreading across his face as he seemed to recognize her. Laura's treacherous heart skipped a beat. The man was entirely too good looking for her peace of mind.

"Good morning." Graham's richly timbred voice greeted her.

Suddenly, inexplicably winded, Laura gasped her reply, "Good morning."

"Mind if I join you?" Graham fell into step with her, matching her pace, even as he asked. Laura shook her head to indicate he was welcome, unwilling to trust her mutinous voice. They ran in silence, their movements perfectly synchronized, their footfalls pounding staccato in the morning quiet.

"How far do you run?" Graham asked, after they had completed several passes.

"I'm taking it easy while on vacation, so I'll do just a couple of miles, five or six tops."

Graham squelched a groan. *Five or six miles is taking it easy? Why hadn't Howard warned him that she was a distance runner?* He grimaced. He hadn't run since college, and even then he hadn't liked it. Already his legs ached and his lungs burned. He glanced heavenward, silently petitioning for strength to endure. Remotest China was looking better all the time.

Finally, after what Graham and his legs deemed to be an eternity, Laura slowed the pace to a walk, and they circled the deck one last time to cool off. By now, there were other passengers out, running and walking the track.

"Have you been running long?" Laura asked amiably, anxious to prove she was capable of intelligent conversation.

"I ran some in college, but I just took it up again." Graham grinned down at her. "Very recently."

All too soon for Laura, they reached the door leading into the hall by her cabin. She didn't feel frightened or threatened by Graham's presence. In fact, she found his presence comforting.

Knowing he was by her side as she ran, matching her stride for stride was wonderful, as though even without speaking they shared some common bond. She hated to leave him.

"Here's the door, guess I'll be going in." Laura tried to hide the disappointment that tinged her voice.

"I was going to grab some breakfast. Wanna join me?"

I'd love to, she thought, her heart soaring momentarily, but dutifully she answered instead, "I need to get back to the room. In case Kathi's looking for me." *After all,* she reminded herself, *Kathi has spoken for Graham, I shouldn't be spending time alone with him.*

"At seven?" Graham gave a low chuckle. "Somehow I doubt it."

He may be naive about romance, Laura thought wryly, *but he sure has Kathi pegged.* Her resolve wavered. Maybe it would be all right to have breakfast with him; after all, Graham was her father's friend. She glanced down at her shirt and shorts and frowned up into Graham's eyes that also seemed to be studying her appearance. The warm approval she saw reflected in his eyes was startling, and she flushed slightly. "I'm afraid I'm not dressed for the dining room."

"Me either," Graham assured her, returning his gaze to meet hers, "but they also serve breakfast out on the deck where we were last night. It's very casual."

Laura demurred. Should she go? On the one hand, she felt guilty about spending time alone with Kathi's beau. Somehow, it seemed disloyal. On the other hand, Kathi wouldn't be up for hours, so she wouldn't have spent the time with Graham anyway. Besides, Laura was famished. She'd have to eat breakfast somewhere, she reasoned, so why not with Graham. After all, she had no designs on him. "If you're sure I won't be an imposition." Laura smiled shyly.

"It'll be great. We'll get a chance to get to know each other a little better; although I feel like I know everything about you." In response to Laura's bewildered expression, he explained, "You're Howard's favorite topic, in case you didn't know."

She hadn't known. The information warmed her heart.

The dining area on the International Deck was practically deserted. Most of the activity stemmed from the efforts of crew members who scurried about doing last-minute cleaning and polishing to ready the ship for the day.

Brightly colored umbrellas provided shade from the already scorching sun for the few patrons seated at the scattered tables. Delicious aromas filled the air, causing Laura's stomach to growl fiercely. Graham heard it and laughed. "We better get you some food. From the sound of things, there's not a moment to lose."

They selected their breakfasts from a sumptuous buffet laid out on long, linen-covered tables standing against the wall. There were mounds of artistically arranged fresh fruit, baskets of fresh baked goods, and chafing dishes filled with steaming hot eggs, bacon, and sausage. There was one whole table filled with nothing but cereal, hundreds of individual boxes of every variety available. It was a mouth-watering smorgasbord, and the two lingered long before making their selections.

Well-filled plates in hand, they chose a table by the railing, with a wonderful view of the sapphire sea. The ocean was calm, with only the churning wake of the ship to disturb its glassy, rolling surface.

Both Graham and Laura were famished and ate with gusto. Between bites, they reminisced about their high school days, and the teachers and acquaintances they shared. The conversation was light, full of laughter, and Laura found to her amazement that she was actually enjoying herself. Graham was so unlike any man she'd ever met. He was so easy to talk to, both a wonderful listener and a terrific storyteller.

When Laura spoke, he listened intently, with piercing gray eyes that seemed to see into the depths of her soul. Those same eyes danced and sparkled with mirth when he assumed the role of speaker, relating humorous episodes from his past.

Instead of being tongue-tied and slightly nauseous, as was her norm around men, Laura contributed willingly to the conversation, even adding an amusing anecdote or two of her own. She felt so at ease with him, as though she'd known him all her life.

Time raced by and Laura reluctantly considered she should return to her cabin. Even though they were just talking, she was suffering renewed qualms about monopolizing his time. He was

Kathi's love interest.

Graham seemed to sense her uneasiness. "You're not leaving yet, are you? You can't leave me now," he cajoled, "I hate to finish my coffee alone." He flashed her his dazzling white smile, and her resolve was lost. After all, she reasoned, only a few minutes more wouldn't matter.

"Has your father told you much about our Bible study?" Graham's voice was deceptively casual. Inwardly, he was anxious about the confrontation he knew to be forthcoming. He wanted to talk with her about his faith, and he knew the time was right, but he wanted so much to do it in a way she would receive. Howard had warned him this was a volatile subject:

"No," Laura shook her head. "To be truthful, I didn't let him." She answered sheepishly, remembering how she had treated her father.

"Oh?" Graham's dark brow quirked upward.

Laura hated to get into this discussion. She had discovered she liked Graham, and she didn't want to be offensive. "You see, I'm not really interested in God." There was no malice in her voice; she merely stated her opinion.

Graham leaned back in his chair, stretching his long legs out before him. "That surprises me, considering your relationship to your mother and what a strong Christian she was." He was deliberately baiting her, hoping to draw some reaction from her so he would know how to proceed.

He got an immediate reaction. Laura's spine stiffened visibly and her mahogany eyes flashed. How dare he bring up her beloved mother! That topic was closed, strictly off limits. "What do you know about my mother, anyway?"

Graham was unruffled by her obvious hostility. "Only what your father has told me. I don't believe I ever had the opportunity to meet her."

"Then let's drop it, okay?" Laura's tone reflected her suppressed anger.

Graham declined to answer, instead he continued to make his point. "Howard told me you two were best friends, and that she practically begged you to become a Christian before she died."

He let the thought dangle, hoping to elicit some discussion. Instead, his partner became silent.

Laura's eyes clouded over as long, forgotten memories came to light. She could see her mother, her beautiful face emaciated as the cancer ravaged through her body. Yet, her dark eyes were serene, in spite of the excruciating pain.

Laura could hear her soft voice, "Laura, honey, you mustn't worry. I'm in God's care and I'm not afraid for myself. He'll never abandon me. But Laura, I am afraid for you. Without making the decision to accept Jesus as your Savior, you are the one in danger."

Laura blinked back tears. Other memories flooded over her. Pictures of her mother trying to explain to her the vast measure of God's love and mercy. Sitting on her bed at Easter, her mother too frail to attend church, listening to her mother describe how Jesus went to the cross to take away the sins of the world. She remembered clearly the glowing look on her mother's face, a look confirming how deeply her mother held her convictions.

Each faded memory was bittersweet. Her gentle mother never lost patience with her, never berated her for her disbelief. Laura knew it had been her dying wish to see her daughter become a Christian, yet she had delayed. She hadn't realized the urgency of the situation. She thought she had more time. And now her mother was gone. Forever.

Hot tears coursed down her face. "Christianity didn't help her a bit, Graham." Her voice was strangely flat, emotionless. "God let her die."

Graham's heart wrenched. He'd meant to spark discussion, but he could see that he'd opened deep wounds. *Father,* he prayed silently, *give me wisdom.* He sat forward and reached across the table to take her trembling hands, but she drew back defensively.

"Maybe you have the wrong idea about Christianity, Laura," Graham spoke in low, soothing tones. "It's not a cure-all. We still have problems like everybody else, even sickness and cancer."

"Then what's the point?" Laura's voice was barely a whisper.

Graham's eyes locked on her liquid brown ones, refusing to let her look away and he smiled tenderly. "Christianity is victory, Laura. Victory over the problems and death. Because we know we don't face them alone. The Bible tells us that He will never leave us or forsake us. That means that God is with us through the problems. And that gives us Christians something you can't get from any other source—real peace."

Confusion crowded Laura's mind. Thoughts and memories tumbled crazily through her head. This man, this new-found friend that had the nerve to question her devotion to her precious mother, was repeating the same words her mother had spoken so many years ago. As an optimistic teenager, she had dismissed them, believing with the naïveté of youth that there was nothing she couldn't handle. Now, after nine long years, they sounded wonderful. But could she trust him? Could she trust God? Her little voice spoke ominously, *Can you trust the one who let her die? Never! Trust no one.*

The confusion intensified until Laura's head ached. Distractedly, she massaged her temples to stop the throbbing pain. She couldn't think, she could scarcely breathe. With tears streaming down her cheeks, Laura struggled to her feet. She made a valiant effort to appear composed, brushing away the tears with the back of her hand and offering a tremulous smile to Graham. "I've got to go. It seems I'm still not ready to discuss religion."

Graham was on his feet instantly. "Don't go. We need to talk. I know I've upset you, but this is so important." He reached out to take her arm, but she pulled away.

"Enough!" she cried. "I don't want to hear any more." She turned and fled into the ship.

Graham dropped into his chair, running his fingers through his hair in frustration. He'd had the chance. He thought he'd seen a spark of understanding flicker in her eyes, but instead she'd run away in anger. He'd blown it. "Forgive me, Father." His whispered plea was carried off on the breeze.

❧

Laura raced to her cabin, as if by sheer speed she could outrun the tumult in her mind. She burst into the room, and stood leaning against the door, gasping for breath. The noise must have disturbed still-slumbering Kathi, who stirred under the covers. Laura was instantly contrite for her reckless behavior. She shouldn't take her frustration out on Kathi.

After a quick shower, Laura moved stealthily through the darkened room, so as not to disturb her sleeping friend, collecting the things she would need for the day. First, she gathered her novel from where it lay on the table and tucked it into her red-striped beach bag. Next, she found her floppy straw hat in the closet and plopped it onto her head.

Just before she left, she located a scrap of paper and scribbled a quick note to Kathi, propping it on the night stand where she would be sure to find it when she awoke.

Satisfied that she had everything she needed, Laura opened the door a crack and peered out into the hall. *All clear. Good.* She was afraid Graham would try to follow her, and he was the last person she wanted to see. Well actually, she thought, it was a toss-up between him and Robert as to who she wanted to see least.

Jamming her hat so far down on her head that it effectively obscured her features from view, she slipped through the door and darted down the hall and into the elevator. Once safely inside the empty elevator, she pulled out her map, consulting it for a secluded area where she could lay out on a lounge chair without being discovered.

Laura eliminated any decks that Graham had taken them to last night as too risky, one of her traveling companions might stumble upon her there. The Sky Deck looked like a safe place, so she disembarked there.

By now, nearly ten o'clock, most of the passengers had awakened to begin their first full day at sea, and the Sky Deck was bustling with activity. As Laura had surmised, the deck was littered with shiny, white, lounge chairs, many of which were already filled by eager sunbathers. She scanned the area. To her delight, she located a vacant chair near the railing, and away from most of the other chairs. She plunked her belongings down into the chair to signify possession and turned to survey the deck.

In the center of the floor, surrounded by umbrella-covered tables and chairs, was a lovely swimming pool with sparkling clear water. Laura perked up. A cool, refreshing swim was just what she needed to get her mind off Graham and his meddling. Luckily, she had brought her bathing suit in the beach bag, and she remembered that she'd passed a ladies' room on the way, where she could change.

In minutes, Laura was floating in the cool water. For a time, she busied herself paddling aimlessly through the water, enjoying the sensation as it washed over her. It wasn't long before the words Graham had spoken earlier that morning played again through her memory, disturbing the tranquility of the pool.

No more. I don't want to hear any more, she thought. In a frantic effort to drown the thoughts whirling in her mind, she swam countless laps, racing back and forth across the pool. When she had thoroughly exhausted herself, her arms and legs limp from exertion, and her tormented mind cleared, she eased out of the water, into a waiting towel, and finally dropped into her lounge chair. She closed her eyes, letting the warm sun caress her face and aching body.

"Would you care for a drink this morning?"

Laura squinted up into the smiling face of a waiter, immaculately dressed in a crisp white uniform, with a tray of frozen drinks balanced in his hand. She was so startled when he spoke, as she had not heard him approach, that she sat there, mute.

"Excuse me, ma'am," he tried again, raising his voice a bit, in case she was hard of hearing. "Would you care for something to drink?"

"I'd love a diet cola, if you could find one." She smiled as she spoke.

The waiter was not proof against a pretty face. He grinned and disappeared with a nod. He returned to her immediately with a tall glass of ice and a can of diet cola.

Laura sighed deeply as she sipped her drink. It went a long way in reviving her tired body, but offered little respite for her mind. While she had been active, she had been able to push the thoughts of Graham and the things he had said out of her mind, but now, when she was still, the disquieting thoughts crept back into the forefront.

He has some nerve, her little voice harassed, *bringing up your mother. He didn't even know her. How could he begin to understand your relationship. How dare he stand in judgment of your actions. To suggest that you let your mother down!*

But I did let her down, Laura countered, *I deliberately delayed making my response to God.*

The little voice would not be stilled. *And look what God had done for her. Nothing. He'd abandoned her. He'd let her die.*

Yes, she'd died, but did He abandon her? The question that had plagued Laura for years echoed through her mind. Had God abandoned her mother? Graham had said that even in suffering, God is always there. Her mother had said the same thing. And he had said something else. Christians have peace. Peace in knowing they don't face trouble alone. *That's true,* Laura thought, *I saw it in my mother. Even as she was dying, she had peace.*

A light went on in the recesses of Laura's mind. Her mother had had peace because she had been assured of God's presence, even to the very end of her life. That peace was proof God had not abandoned her. He had stayed by her side. No wonder her mother had smiled fearlessly in the face of death. She had known she didn't face it alone.

That revelation ignited a spark of hope within Laura. *Peace comes from God. And I need peace.* A troubled sigh escaped from Laura. *I wonder if after all this time He would still be willing to give it to me.*

❧

"Where have you been?" Kathi stood in the doorway of the cabin, hands on her hips, and a stern expression on her face. "I was beginning to worry about you." The merry twinkle in her blue eyes gave her away. "Let me guess. You've been holed up somewhere with a book, haven't you?"

Laura nodded guiltily, clutching her paperback to her chest. "I'm sorry I've been gone all day. I hope I haven't spoiled your plans."

"Nonsense!" Kathi's eyes glowed brightly. "I had a wonderful afternoon with Graham. I'm afraid you ruined Robert's plans though. He wore me out asking about you, where you were, and when you'd be back."

"I'm so sorry, I just didn't think."

"Are you kidding? Your strategy was terrific. Keeping a man waiting is a wonderful way to pique his interest. You're a natural flirt," Kathi proclaimed with obvious pride.

Laura rolled her eyes. "Somehow I doubt it," she mumbled. Kathi had completely misinterpreted her actions, but Laura had no intention of correcting her. She walked over to her bed and dropped her things on it in a heap.

Kathi tagged along behind her, and perched on the end of the bed. "Why, he's chomping at the bit to see you." She giggled delightedly, rubbing her hands together. "He'll just have to wait till dinner. By the way, Graham said he'd pick us up at eight."

"No!" Laura answered sharply. She quickly amended her tone, trying to sound cheerful. "What I mean is, I'll go to dinner with Robert tonight, if you don't mind."

The knowing grin on Kathi's face indicated that she believed Laura preferred Robert's company, confirming her romantic notions about the two of them. Laura hated to mislead her, but she couldn't tell her the truth. Anyway, she reasoned, this would allow Kathi to pursue Graham with a clear conscience.

Truthfully, the idea of going to dinner with Robert as her date was unpleasant, but facing Graham after this morning would be worse. She had made a total fool of herself, getting so emotional in front of him. She was certain he was as disgusted with her as she was disgusted with herself, and she couldn't bear to see rejection in his gray eyes.

Laura felt a tug at her heart. She wanted release from the isolation that held her prisoner. She had risked opening up to Graham, exposing a little of her vulnerability to him, sensing that in him she would find a friend. But then, at the crucial point, she had given in to cowardice and stalked off in tears. She'd had her chance and she had blown it. Now he would want nothing to do with her. And that hurt. She could hear her little voice gloating. *You are a fool. With friendship comes pain. You are all alone.*

The shrill ring of the telephone startled her back from her thoughts. She leaned over and picked up the receiver.

"Laura, is that you?" She recognized Robert's voice on the line. "It's Robert Gleason," he paused, "You know, from last night."

Laura smiled in spite of herself. He must have the idea she had so many suitors that she had difficulty keeping track of them all. That idea struck her as funny. First, Kathi pronounces her a natural flirt, and then Robert assumes she may have forgotten him amidst all her other conquests. *If only they knew.* She stifled a giggle that bubbled up within her, and her brown eyes sparkled with mirth.

Kathi, who was sitting beside her, intently studying her face for clues to the conversation, saw the delighted look and beamed. Laura was in love. And her matchmaking efforts had been the cause. This surpassed her wildest dreams. Now if only she could convince Graham to follow suit.

"Yes, Robert, I remember you," Laura replied pleasantly, her smile reflected in her voice.

Robert sounded relieved. "I've been trying to find you all day. Can I see you tonight?"

Laura avoided the implied question of where she had been and answered smoothly, "That would be lovely. Suppose you swing by here about 7:45, and you and I can go to dinner together." Laura surprised herself with how easily the words flowed from her mouth, as if she were experienced in this sort of thing. Kathi glowed at her, nodding in approval, as a teacher might encourage a budding pupil.

"That'll be great. See you then."

Laura replaced the receiver and closed her eyes. *How do I get myself into these messes,* she wondered. The confidence she displayed on the phone was short-lived, and even now her stomach churned and her palms grew clammy at the thought of her upcoming date.

nine

Two minutes before Robert was due to arrive, Laura's confidence was in shambles. Despite Kathi's enthusiastic approval of her appearance, and reassurance that they'd all be sitting together in the dining room, she felt an uncontrollable urge to lock herself in the bathroom for the night.

"He'll be here in just a minute," Kathi announced cheerfully from the dressing table. She had appointed herself timekeeper and had called out the time in regular intervals for the last hour, fraying Laura's already unsteady nerves.

"Terrific," Laura whispered sarcastically to her reflection in the full-length mirror on the closet door. She studied the image with interest. The young woman before her showed no signs of nervousness. If anything, she was the picture of cool sophistication. Aloof. Untouchable.

She wore a black damask suit with a short, fitted jacket and a slim skirt. The front of the jacket was adorned with five large rhinestone-studded buttons, giving it a dressy look. Her mass of golden hair was upswept into an elegant coiffure and her only accessories were simple diamond earrings and the diamond bracelet at her wrist. Since inwardly she bore no resemblance to the calm façade she saw reflected, she concluded wryly that it must be true that clothes do make the woman.

Promptly at 7:45 there was a sharp knock at the door. Laura took a deep, steadying breath, squared her slender shoulders, and proceeded to the door, much the way a condemned prisoner would approach the electric chair. "This isn't fatal, this isn't fatal, this isn't fatal," she repeated softly. Drying her palms one last time on her skirt, she swung open the door to face her companion for the evening.

Robert broke into a wide smile when he saw her, and he stepped forward, arms outstretched, to greet her.

Reflexively, Laura offered her hand for a handshake. "Good evening, Robert. It's good to see you again." She used the same formal tone with him that she applied in business situations, hoping to insure that their relationship remained platonic.

Robert was not offended by the cool reception; in fact, he did not seem to notice. For a moment, he stood transfixed, his dark eyes moving slowly over every inch of her, studying her from head to toe, a wolfish grin signaling his approval. Laura fought the urge to run.

He failed to release her hand after the handshake; instead, he held it tenderly and moving forward, he casually slipped it through his arm.

"Shall we go?" He smiled warmly into her eyes.

Laura returned the smile, with effort. "Yes, I'm ready." *As ready as I'll ever be,* she thought.

Robert guided her down the hall, her arm held possessively in his, and they stepped into the waiting elevator.

Graham had rounded the corner of the hall from the opposite side, just in time to see Robert and Laura at the girls' door. He backed up slightly, so as not to be seen. Ordinarily, he was not given to spying, but he decided to tread lightly until he knew the best way to approach Laura after this morning's fiasco.

He knew she was furious with him, not that he blamed her. He'd handled things so badly. The thought that she was angry with him was strangely discomforting, and he had spent a significant portion of his day considering ways to make amends.

From his vantage point, Graham was unable to hear their conversation, but he could see clearly that Laura's arm was entwined with Robert's and his head was intimately close to hers.

A sharp jab that felt suspiciously like jealousy impaled him. *Jealous of Robert? Certainly not.* Graham dismissed the impertinent thought immediately. His only interest in Laura was her immortal soul. True, he had noticed that she was beautiful, intelligent, and sensitive, but that was of no consequence to him. His involvement was strictly her spiritual well-being.

Nonetheless, it was annoying to see the two of them standing so close together, practically in each other's arms. *And what in the world could Robert possibly be saying that would cause Laura to smile like that?*

Graham was still stewing when he reached the girls' cabin. He knocked once before the door burst open and an excited Kathi burst out, colliding with his chest.

"Oh Graham, you're here." She stepped back and smiled up into his face. "You've just missed Laura, I'm afraid. She and Robert have already headed off for dinner." She wiggled her eyebrows, insinuating there was much more to the story and that she was dying to tell it.

Graham frowned slightly, his dark brows furrowed. "Did you tell her that I planned to take you both down to dinner?"

"Sure!" Kathi said brightly. "But she insisted she'd prefer to go on with Robert. I guess they wanted to be alone." She giggled, unaware of the scowl marring Graham's features. "Isn't it just so wonderful? A shipboard romance." She smiled meaningfully into his face.

"Yeah, wonderful," Graham repeated without enthusiasm. "Just wonderful."

Dinner dragged on interminably for Laura. The delicious meal consisted of broiled fish with a light herb sauce, surrounded by an array of colorful steamed vegetables, but she only picked at her food. The combination of nervousness about Robert and the nearness of Graham dealt a deathblow to her appetite. Robert and Kathi carried the conversation aptly, each relating amusing stories from their past, and Laura smiled and laughed at the appropriate places, but her mind was elsewhere.

From the moment Kathi and Graham entered the dining room, her thoughts were centered on him. She knew it was wrong, Kathi had spoken for him, and she was being disloyal, but her stubborn mind refused to cooperate.

He looked impossibly handsome this evening, she noted with a surreptitious glance, his chiseled features golden bronzed from his day in the sun. He wore a dark suit that draped his broad shoulders splendidly, with a crisp white shirt and a silk tie the color of his eyes. His dark hair curled slightly at his collar, inviting curious fingers to run through its thick waves.

Enough! She chastised her wayward thoughts. *He belongs to my best friend. Besides, I'm not interested in him, at least not other than for a friend. And I ruined that opportunity this morning with my emotional outburst.* With that sobering reminder, she reined in her imaginations and tried to redirect them toward Robert.

Robert is nice. And I think he is considerate, and I have always liked brown eyes. Just that quickly, her imagination conjured up visions of steely gray eyes, holding her captive in their regard. Eyes sparkling with laughter. Eyes glowing with compassion. Eyes that were strictly off limits.

So it went the entire evening. She would reel in her thoughts, focus them on her escort, and they would immediately be drawn, as if by a magnet, back to the man sitting across from her. The man whose gaze she dared not meet, lest she find the rejection there that she feared most of all. The man who belonged to her best friend.

When the waiter finally began to clear away the dessert dishes, Laura was in a state of mental exhaustion. Cerebral volleyball was strenuous. She didn't want to think anymore. Not about Robert, not about Graham, not about anything. All she wanted to do was crawl into bed, pull her covers up tightly under her chin and close her eyes in sleep. She pushed back her chair with the intention of excusing herself for the evening, when Robert spoke.

"It's too early to call it a night. What do you say we all catch the play in the theater. It's supposed to be quite a performance." Robert looked over at Laura, awaiting her response.

Kathi was quicker. She seemed to sense that Laura was about to call a premature end to the evening, so she answered hastily, "That sounds great. Don't you think so, Graham?" She flashed him a coy smile. He had been disturbingly distant for the entire meal. She needed more time to help him realize how much he cared for her.

"Fine by me."

"Laura, what about you? You haven't said much all evening. Do you want to see the show or would you prefer something quieter, just the two of us?" Robert lowered his voice slightly, making the question sound more intimate.

What a choice, Laura thought. *Like a condemned person being able to select the means by which he is killed.* It was painfully obvious she wasn't going to get back up to her cabin anytime soon and while she didn't know what "something quieter, just the two of us" meant, she was certain she didn't want any part of that. So the decision was simple.

"I love the theater," she said, a little too emphatically. She flushed and lowered her voice, "A play sounds great."

The four of them arrived at the crowded theater just as the house lights flickered, indicating the performance was about to begin. A uniformed usher at the door informed them they were indeed fortunate, there were still a few seats available, but not four together. Laura beamed. That was the first good news she'd had all night. She could actually enjoy the show if she sat by herself, away from her distracting companions. She felt like jumping up and down, clapping her hands.

Graham saw the wide smile on her face and assumed it was because she wanted to be alone with Robert. Away from him. A now familiar ache settled in his chest.

Throughout dinner, he'd watched her, searching for some indication that she had forgiven him, but he had found none. She had ignored him completely, as if he were too horrible to even look at, and instead, doted on Robert, saving her beguiling smile for him alone. Not that he was jealous, of course, he assured himself. He merely felt an obligation to clear up their earlier misunderstanding.

The usher led Laura and Robert in first, and seated them together, much to Laura's chagrin. Their seats were in the second row, on the aisle. Kathi and Graham were seated in the back of the auditorium, in the middle of the last row.

Almost immediately, the houselights faded and the curtain

opened. Robert's arm found its way around Laura, possessively encircling the back of her seat. The familiarity of the action made her uncomfortable, but there was little she could do without causing an undue disturbance, so she perched rigidly on the end of her chair, refusing to lean back into the curve of his arm.

Laura had always loved the theater, but tonight, even the elaborate scenery and beautiful costumes failed to hold her attention. Her mind wandered back to the morning, to the things Graham had said, and to the way he had looked at her. If she closed her eyes, she could see him grinning as clearly as if he were seated beside her. She was so restless, it was difficult to sit still.

The first act was barely completed when Laura turned to Robert. "Would you excuse me?" she whispered. "I need to, uh, to go to the ladies' room." He nodded absently, his attention riveted on the players on stage.

She slipped down the darkened aisle and through the double door without a sound. Once outside, she exhaled deeply. She had escaped. The usher that had seated her earlier eyed her quizzically. "Are you ill?"

"Ill?" Laura felt so relieved that she giggled. "No, I just came out for a little fresh air. It's a bit stuffy inside." It was evident the usher was unconvinced by her explanation as he continued to study her for signs of seasickness.

She gave him a cheery smile and headed down the hall. Belatedly, she realized she did not have her map with her, nor did she have a clue as to how to get outside from here. She knew she couldn't be gone too long, or Robert would start to worry, but these stolen minutes were sweet. She walked slowly down the thickly carpeted hall, savoring the freedom of being alone.

At the end of the long corridor, she stopped at a door she assumed would open to the stairs. Stairs that would likely lead to an outside deck. She reached out to grasp the knob when two strong arms planted themselves firmly on the door, one on either side of her, trapping her.

"Laura, we've got to talk." A deep voice, velvety smooth, whispered in her ear, sending tiny shivers down her spine.

With a gasp, Laura whirled around and found herself face to face with Graham. "Graham, you startled me," she whispered breathlessly. "I didn't hear you coming."

"I know. I was afraid you'd run if you knew I was behind you."

Laura raised questioning brown eyes to meet his, expecting to find mirth reflected in their silvery depths. There was none. His eyes were solemn, as was the expression on his face. "Why would I run from you?" she asked, genuinely perplexed. "After the way I acted this morning, I would expect you to run from me."

Graham could scarcely believe his ears. She thought he was angry with her. His voice was husky with emotion. "I never intended to hurt you, but I'm afraid that my reckless speech this morning dredged up painful memories. Will you please forgive me?"

Laura was incredulous. "You aren't angry?" Her soft mahogany eyes were wide with amazement.

"Angry?" He wanted to laugh. He had to fight the urge to gather her in his arms and hold her close, cradling her against his chest. He lowered his arms that still pinned her to the door and clenched and unclenched his fists, straining to keep from touching her. His deep voice was barely a whisper, "I could never be angry with you."

Laura drew in a deep breath to bolster her courage. "Then can we be friends?" she asked with the innocence and hopeful intensity of a child.

The urgent plea tugged at Graham's heartstrings. Again, he had to resist the overwhelming desire to sweep her into his arms. For a moment, his arms seemed to have developed a mind of their own, and he shoved his hands deep into his pockets for restraint. He chuckled, "Yes, Laura, we can be friends."

The tender smile he gave her caused Laura's heart to skip a beat. She was consumed with the sudden need to throw her arms around him. Only by clasping her hands firmly behind her back could she trust herself not to do it. They stood there, face to face, unmoving. The air was charged with electricity.

"There you are! The usher told me you came this way." Robert rushed anxiously toward Laura. "I was beginning to worry about you." It wasn't until then that he seemed to notice Graham. "Graham, nice of you to look out for her." Robert studied the flushed face and overly bright eyes of his date with concern. He stepped between the two and took Laura's arm, possessively tucking it through his. "You look tired, Laura. I'll get you back to the cabin just as soon as the play is over." He cast a suspicious glance at Graham as he began to lead her away. As an afterthought, he called over his shoulder, "See you later, Graham."

Laura followed him obediently back into the auditorium, too happy to care that she wasn't the least bit interested in the play. She felt as if the weight of the world had been lifted from her shoulders. *He's not angry with me. He wants to be my friend.* Laura sank back into her chair and sighed contentedly.

Robert glanced over when he heard the sigh and was pleased to see a smile on her lips. He found her very desirable, and it was apparent she returned his feelings. The thought of getting her alone, someplace away from her chaperone, brought a wide smile to his face.

The curtain closed a final time to the thunderous applause of the audience and the house lights came up. Robert deftly maneuvered them through the milling crowd and out into the hall, exiting well ahead of the others.

True to his word, he headed straight for her cabin. Her initial delight was cut short by the realization that tonight she was going to receive a good night kiss, whether she wanted it or not. And she did not. There would be no Graham at the door to intimidate her ardent suitor tonight. He and Kathi were no doubt still waiting to exit the auditorium. Her stomach felt slightly queasy and her palms grew moist. Tonight there would be no escape.

The elevator stopped on the Olympic Deck, and Robert and she alighted together. Laura walked slowly, trying to delay the inevitable. She toyed nervously with the diamond bracelet glittering on her wrist. Rounding the corner to her cabin, Laura stopped in her tracks. She blinked and, unsure that what she saw was not a figment of her imagination, she blinked again.

Leaning against the wall by her door in comfortable repose, ankles crossed, stood Graham Kirkland. Laura stifled a giggle of relief. He had done it again. She didn't know how he had managed it, but he'd saved her again.

Robert groaned almost imperceptibly. "Father Graham appears to be waiting up," he muttered under his breath.

Graham stepped forward to greet the advancing couple. He had to swallow the laughter rising in his throat at the sight of Robert's face. It was apparent by his irritated expression that Graham had arrived in time to spoil Robert's plans for a romantic farewell.

"Thanks, Robert, I appreciate you looking out for her. After what you said earlier about Laura being overtired, I thought I better check up on her before she retires for the evening, just to be certain she's not ill." Graham spoke in a fatherly tone, trying desperately not to smile. He placed a hand on Laura's shoulder and steered her toward the cabin door. "You hurry on in and get a good night's rest. We'll see you in the morning." He opened the door for her and scooted her inside, but not before she caught a glimpse of what she thought was a twinkle in his eyes.

"Good night, Robert," she called through the door, before Graham could pull it closed. To be polite she added, "I had a lovely evening."

Laura leaned back against the closed door and giggled softly.

"What's going on?" Kathi demanded crossly, her hands waving furiously through the air.

"I'm not sure I know what you mean."

"Why in the world did Graham drag me out of the theater like we were fleeing from a fire, practically carry me up two flights of stairs, and shove me into this room like baggage? Are we under attack?"

"Attack? Like from pirates? I hardly think so." Laura laughed at her disgruntled friend. "As far as why he rushed you up here, I'm not certain." Did she dare to hope he had come up to rescue her? Not likely. He probably had come to determine whether or not she was ill, just as he'd said. After all, Howard had made him responsible for her well being. It wouldn't sit well with her father if she came down sick, and nothing had been done.

"A perfect night wasted," Kathi pouted. "Did you know there is a full moon out tonight? They are very romantic, you know. I was counting on taking a long walk with Graham under the stars to solidify our relationship."

Kathi balked after she spoke. She had deliberately given Laura the impression that there was more to their relationship than there really was, which she knew now was untrue. She'd never lied to Laura before. But this was important. She couldn't let Laura suspect that she and Graham weren't an item. Otherwise, Laura would feel obligated to entertain Graham, since he was her father's friend, and that could possibly jeopardize her relationship with Robert.

Kathi couldn't let that happen. It had taken Laura a long time to fall in love, and Kathi would do all in her power to protect her best friend's happiness. A little white lie was harmless enough. Besides, she was an eternal optimist. Maybe Graham would come to realize what a great pair they made. Maybe he just needed more time.

"I'm sorry, Kathi, I really don't know what he was thinking. I guess I'll never understand men."

Long after the lights were out and the room was blanketed in comforting darkness, Laura lay in bed, replaying the day's events over and over.

She was still troubled by the memories of how deeply she'd disappointed her beloved mother. And many unanswered questions still danced in her head. Peace continued to elude her. But tonight, the suffocating black pall that had hung over her for years was lifting. She had risked opening up and exposing her vulnerability. She had asked Graham to be a friend. She had lowered her armor of isolation, and it felt good.

She snuggled deeply under the covers. In the back of her mind, she could hear the words Graham had spoken earlier. "The Bible tells us that He will never leave us or forsake us. That means that God is with us through the problems. And that gives us Christians something you can't get from any other source—real peace." Clinging to those words as to a lifeline, Laura drifted off to sleep.

⮞

"Father," Graham confessed as he knelt stiffly by his bed, "Again I come to You for forgiveness. Rather than trusting You today, I took matters into my own hands. Through my efforts, I was able to alienate the one person that You've asked me to minister to. I am reminded of the scripture that says if I am faithful to confess my sins, that You are faithful to forgive me. I accept Your forgiveness with gratitude.

"Thank you, Father, for allowing me a second chance. Thanks, too, for the forgiveness I found in Laura's eyes tonight. Help me, Lord, to be worthy of Your call."

Graham rose painfully to his feet, his long legs stiff and sore from the miles he'd logged that morning. He paused, and as an afterthought, he sat down on the edge of the bed, bowed his head once more and prayed.

"One more thing, Father. It's about Laura. I'm struggling with some feelings for her that I don't understand. I came here to teach her about You, to be a friend to her. Suddenly, I find being a friend isn't quite enough.

"I know Your Word teaches that believers must not be unequally yoked with unbelievers, so she's definitely not right for me." He sighed. "Then, there's the matter of Robert. Kathi says Laura is crazy about him. And I am certainly not interested in stealing another man's girl. I know You've got strong opinions about that, too. But I just can't get her out of my mind. She's special, Father, really special. I don't even know how to pray about this mess, so I'm turning my feelings about her over to You. Help me to honor You." Graham chuckled softly, "Oh, and I'm sorry for meddling with Robert and Laura tonight." He paused momentarily, remembering the look on Robert's face. "Actually, I guess I need Your forgiveness because I'm not really sorry at all; it felt great. Your will be done."

ten

Laura hopped out of bed at 6 A.M. sharp. She'd been lying there, wide awake, for almost an hour, watching the time tick away on the clock, unable to go back to sleep. Without making a sound, she gathered her running clothes and slipped into the bathroom to dress, careful not to awaken Kathi. In a flash she emerged, dressed and ready for her morning run.

She couldn't remember ever looking forward to exercise like she was this morning, and a shy grin crept over her face as she considered the reason why today was different. *Graham.* She was looking forward to spending time with Graham.

She battled the guilty feeling that she was being disloyal to Kathi. *After all,* she told herself, *I'm not romantically involved with him. We're just friends. Even though he is the most wonderful man I've ever met, and my heart does flipflops when I see him, it doesn't mean that I feel anything more than friendship for him. He's Kathi's. We're just friends.*

Laura pushed open the heavy door leading outside and stepped into the morning mists. The breeze swirled playfully about her, teasing her with its salty spray. She walked to the railing and stood staring into the gently rolling sea. In the silence of the early morning, studying the vastness of the open sea, Laura caught a glimpse of the tranquility that had eluded her all these years. If only she knew how to make it hers.

She suddenly felt self-conscious, just standing there, obviously waiting for Graham. *What if he preferred to run alone. Or even worse, what if he did not come at all. He'd never actually said he'd be there.* Laura's heart sank with the thought.

If he did come, she was determined he would not find her waiting. He might get the wrong idea. He might think she was interested in him for more than just friendship. Which she wasn't. He was Kathi's.

She warmed up quickly and sprinted off. Her long strides were punctuated by the rhythmic beat of her tennis shoes on the glossy planks. To her ears, the solitary footfalls sounded very much alone.

Laura completed her fifth lap with a dejected sigh. *No Graham.* Each time she rounded the track, passing the doors leading inside, she watched expectantly, hoping to see his tall, handsome frame leaning up against the wall, waiting for her. And each time she passed she was more disappointed.

For the first few laps, she was able to console herself that he had just gotten a late start, and he'd be there any minute. By the fifth lap, she resigned herself to the truth. He wasn't coming. She ran by the door the fifth time, picking up speed. Her disappointment seemed to fuel her energy and her feet were fairly flying along. But not her heart. It was grounded.

&

Graham eased out the door, every muscle in his body screaming in agony. Muscles hurt that he wasn't aware he had. He'd seriously considered staying in bed this morning; he wasn't at all certain that his legs would take the punishment of another day of running. But something compelled him on. He told himself it was the zeal he felt for sharing God's word. That was true, but inwardly, he knew it was more. It was the memory of dark brown eyes framed with thick brown lashes that beckoned him.

He knew that she was another's, and he vowed he would do nothing to interfere, he simply wanted to be with her. To look into her eyes, to feel the warmth of her smile. She said she wanted to be friends. That would be enough.

Laura saw him standing at the door. Even halfway down the track, there was no mistaking those broad shoulders or that impressive height. It was Graham. She continued running, trying her best to appear casual, but her heart thumped wildly in her chest. She could scarcely contain her delight. An enormous smile covered her face. "Good morning!" she called cheerfully, still several paces away.

"Good morning to you." He looked past her, as if he expected to see something. "Somebody chasing you?" he teased, noting the speed at which she was running.

Laura flushed bright red. "Got carried away I guess." She slowed her pace, and he loped to her side.

They ran in companionable silence for a time, moving as one around the empty track, each satisfied just to be together.

"Have you hurt your leg?" Laura asked, interrupting the quiet. He was keeping up the pace, but she noticed he didn't run with the fluid grace he'd exhibited yesterday. He almost acted like he was in pain.

"It's nothing really," Graham gritted out. "A little early morning stiffness, that's all. Old age must be setting in," he joked.

Laura was concerned. "Would you prefer to stop?"

"When you're ready." He smiled hopefully.

"Actually, a good run is probably just what you need to work out the stiffness," Laura said after giving the matter some consideration. "At least, that's what my coach used to say. I'll bet after another couple of miles, you'll be as good as new."

Or dead, Graham thought grimly.

Three long miles later, Laura slowed to a brisk walk. "Feeling better?" she inquired, studying his handsome face for the answer.

"I sure don't feel like I did when I started," Graham replied honestly. Though he wouldn't have believed it possible, he felt worse.

Laura smiled in satisfaction, pleased that her advice had worked so well.

In spite of his suffering, Graham found he did not want to leave her. "If I promise not to be offensive, will you join me for breakfast?" he asked. "That is if you don't have other plans," he amended, as it occurred to him that she might prefer to dine with Robert.

"No plans, and breakfast sounds terrific. I'm famished."

Graham flashed her a heart-stopping smile, and painfully led the way to the deck below.

The breakfast buffet offered a similar assortment of mouth-watering entrées to the buffet yesterday. Laura chose a flaky cheese

Danish and a plate of fresh strawberries, while Graham ordered an omelet. They found an empty table by the railing and sat down, this time on the opposite end of the deck, both wanting to avoid any reminder of yesterday's altercation.

Having eaten so little the night before, Laura was exceptionally hungry and attacked her breakfast with relish. She polished off the Danish and berries in record time. It wasn't until she popped the last juicy strawberry into her mouth that she noticed her companion had barely touched his breakfast. He seemed far more intent upon watching her.

"Is something wrong?" she asked, strangely pleased by his attention.

Graham faltered, embarrassed that he had been caught staring. After all, she belonged to another. It was just so difficult to look away from those engaging brown eyes. "Wrong? No, not at all. I guess I was just daydreaming."

"You know, Graham, there's something I'd like to ask you, if it's not too personal."

Graham nodded for her to continue.

"You never told me why you became a Christian."

Graham's brow arched in question. He was astonished to hear her bring up Christianity. He had already resigned himself to the fact that he would not mention the subject again, but would wait until she broached the topic before he said any more. He honestly hadn't expected it to come up at all.

Laura saw the look and giggled shyly. "Don't be afraid, I promise I won't run away. Honest, I'm truly interested."

Graham studied the expectant face before him, trying to assess her sincerity. The look in her big brown eyes said it all. She was ready to listen.

"My family are all committed Christians, so I was raised around it. It seemed natural to me." He paused, and gave her a meaningful look. "Of course, you and I both know that having Christian parents, or even attending church doesn't make one a Christian. You have to personally accept Jesus Christ as your Savior. I didn't make that personal commitment to Jesus until my freshman year in college." He stopped for a moment and looked out toward the horizon.

Laura mistook his silence as an indication that he was finished. She hadn't gotten the answers she was seeking. "You haven't told me why you are a Christian."

Graham smiled at her persistence, exposing his perfect white teeth. The smile carried all the way to his eyes causing them to sparkle with merriment. Tiny little laugh lines formed at the corners. Laura wished he wouldn't do that. She could hardly concentrate on what he was saying.

"I finally figured I couldn't do it alone. And believe me, I tried." He chuckled at the memory. "I found out quickly that life can be difficult, full of challenges and disappointments, and I recognized that I couldn't handle it on my own. And I wanted the peace you and I talked about yesterday, God's peace."

Graham hesitated. He was afraid he'd overwhelm her with his sermon, but there was so much more to tell. He didn't want to turn her off with preachiness. Should he quit now and continue at another time? Would there even be another time?

He tossed a quick, silent prayer toward heaven, asking for direction. His answer was immediate. Suddenly, he knew he must add just one more thing. "You know, I haven't mentioned one of the biggest selling features of Christianity. Only Christianity offers the additional benefit of eternal life."

Laura nodded. "My mother mentioned eternal life several times before she died." A lump formed in her throat as she admitted, "though I never really listened to what she said."

Graham reached across the table and gently took Laura's hand. "Eternal life means that even after our physical bodies die, our spirits will live on forever, with God. So one day we will be reunited with our loved ones in heaven, a place where there is no death or suffering. Your mother is already there, with Jesus. Someday, I'll get to meet her there."

Tears welled up in Laura's eyes. Everything Graham said spoke directly to her aching heart. The words were balm to her wounded spirit. She wanted the peace that came from the assurance that she didn't face life alone. She needed it. And to think that she could see her mother again, that was almost too good to be true.

"Do you think God would let me become a Christian? After all the times I rejected Him in the past?" Laura asked with a catch in her throat.

Graham smiled tenderly. "He's waiting with open arms."

"How do I do it?" she whispered softly.

"It's so simple, Laura. All you have to do is ask. Tell God you realize you can't do it alone, you know that He sent His only Son to die for your sins, and you accept Jesus as your Savior. Confess it with your mouth and believe it with your heart. That's all there is to it." A joyous smile stretched across his face. "Are you ready to ask Him?"

"Hi, you two!" Kathi bounded over to the table, her dark curls blowing in the breeze. "I'm not interrupting anything, am I?" She looked at Laura and then over at Graham. "What in the world is going on? You two look so serious. Did they announce there wouldn't be seconds on dessert tonight?" She giggled at her own joke.

Laura guiltily withdrew her hand from under Graham's. "We were just talking, that's all. In fact, I need to go. No doubt Robert will be looking for me." She stood up from the table and smiled weakly. "If you two will excuse me."

"Ah, young love," Kathi sighed as she watched her friend enter the ship. "Isn't it romantic?" She turned bright blue eyes to Graham. "I wanted to surprise you by meeting you for breakfast, although how anyone can eat at eight o'clock in the morning is beyond me." She twirled around on her toes. "Well, are you surprised?"

Graham's reply was less than enthusiastic. "You'll never know how much."

No sooner was Laura inside the door to the ship when the assault began. *You aren't really considering becoming a Christian are you?* her little voice demanded. *You can't possibly believe all that tripe. God doesn't care about you. And why would you want Him to? He cared for your mother and let her die.* The familiar words reverberated through her mind. *You've got to make it alone,* the voice hissed vehemently. *You can't trust anyone but yourself. They'll hurt you. You've got to go it alone.*

Laura smiled to herself. She responded with an assurance long sought, but never before realized. *Yes, I believe it all. I've tried making it alone, and my life has been a complete disaster. But no more. I won't be alone any more, because today I'm going to become a Christian. And then, come what may, God and I will face it together.*

Once back at her cabin, Laura knelt at the side of her bed as she remembered seeing her precious mother do so many years before. "God," she prayed humbly, "it's me, Laura Wells. It's been an awfully long time since we last talked. I'm ready to make a decision now, the one I should have made years ago." She sighed deeply, remembering the hopeful look glowing in her mother's eyes, while she presented the gospel to her daughter. She'd died with that hopeful look, never seeing her hope fulfilled.

"I am a sinner and not worthy to become Your child, I know that. I also know You love me, and You sent Jesus to bear the punishment I deserve, so I could become Your child. I'm ready. I accept Jesus' sacrifice. I make Him my Savior." A slow smile crept across her face.

No lightning bolts crashed through the room. No choir of angels appeared at the foot of the bed, singing a heavenly chorus. In fact, the room was silent. But Laura knew at once that her prayer had been answered. The dull ache she had known as a constant companion for nine long years was gone. In its place was an indescribable warmth. Laura recognized it instantly. It was peace.

"Thank You, God. Thank You for eternal life. Thanks for the promise that I'll see my mom again." Laura began to rise but stopped midway. "Oh, and God, thank You so much for not abandoning her. She knew it all along, and now I know it too."

eleven

Laura trotted up to the sun deck without a care in the world. Kathi and Graham were together already, so there was no need for her to sacrifice her day entertaining Robert. Although, unaccountably, the picture of the two of them together caused a slight twinge in her chest and a catch in her throat. It wasn't that she didn't want them to be together, it was just that. . .

Enough of this useless introspection, she chastised herself. She was free to do as she pleased, which was to lie out in the hot Caribbean sun and finish her book. She knew that since her mind was uncluttered with its usual turmoil, she would be able to read and enjoy the novel.

In the event that Robert took it upon himself to locate her, Laura took the precaution of choosing a well-hidden chair, one that afforded her a clear view of who was approaching. Just in case she had to make a quick exit.

She dropped into the chair, arranging her things beside her. The waiter she recognized from yesterday materialized at her side and placed in her hand a tall glass of ice and a can of diet cola. Laura smiled. "You remembered. How thoughtful you are." She reached into her bag and pulled out a dollar bill to tip him. "Thank you so much."

The waiter sauntered off cheerfully. A nice tip and a smile from a beautiful woman made the monotony of his job a lot more palatable.

The sun was no longer overhead, but had begun its descent when Laura closed the cover of her book with a deep contented sigh. She loved a happy ending. She noticed the crowd on the deck was starting to thin out, and she suspected that it must be getting late. A quick glance at the watch in her bag confirmed she had been gone too long. Without delay, she packed her things in her beach bag and padded across the deck, into the ship.

Kathi opened the door for her before she could turn the key in the lock. "I'm so glad you're here. It's been so awful." Her voice rose as she waved her arm dramatically.

Laura panicked. "What's so awful? Are you hurt?"

Kathi moaned with despair. "No, I'm not hurt. I'm frustrated. I can't decide what to wear to the captain's reception tonight." She led Laura over to the closet. "I need something to dazzle Graham tonight. Would I be more successful in red sequins or pink bugle beads?"

The look on her face was so forlorn that Laura had to laugh. "You practically frighten me out of my wits because you can't choose a dress? I could throttle you." She hugged her friend who seemed to be on the verge of tears. "I'm only teasing. These clothing decisions must not be entered into lightly."

Laura peered into the closet. "Let's see now, the pink or the red." She paused in thoughtful consideration. "You look especially striking in the red. It brings out your beautiful coloring. But I like the pink one; too, it's so feminine." She turned to Kathi. "In my opinion, if you want to knock his socks off, go with the red."

Kathi smiled in relief. "I knew you'd know. You're terrific with tough decisions." A sudden frown marred her face. "But what about you? What will you wear tonight? The captain's reception is black tie—very dressy. This is your chance to really shine with Robert. I have found that with some men, all it takes is the right outfit to make them declare their intentions."

Laura grimaced at the mention of Robert's name and the thought of him declaring any intentions at all. Shining for him was the very last thing she wanted to do. She preferred that he keep his distance. She wondered if now was a good time to tell Kathi her true feelings for Robert. Or rather, her true lack of feelings. It would certainly get her off the hook.

Twice she opened her mouth to speak, but both times she stopped short. She couldn't bring herself to do it. It was such a small request Kathi had made of her, to keep occupied with Robert and allow her some uninterrupted time with Graham, it seemed hopelessly selfish to refuse.

Besides, Laura thought, it would probably be worse if she admitted the truth. Knowing how considerate Graham was, it would be just as Kathi had said. If he knew she wasn't interested in Robert, he would insist she accompany them everywhere, and that was one threesome Laura wanted no part of. She wasn't sure why, but the concept of watching the two of them together, falling in love, was disturbing.

It's not as though I'm suffering, Laura reminded herself. Unless you counted the fact that going out with Robert made her a nervous wreck. Or that she had nearly ruined two expensive outfits by wiping perspiration-drenched hands on them. Those were such minor things compared to her best friend's happiness. *No,* she decided firmly, *I'll play along with it.*

Kathi was standing at the door of Laura's closet, rummaging through the clothes. She stood back, studying the contents for a moment. "Did you know that practically all your clothes are black or navy?"

Laura hadn't noticed before. She shrugged indifferently. "I like basic colors, I guess."

"That's the accountant in you speaking. What about the woman in you? Have you ever considered buying something in a cheerful color, like pink or yellow?"

"Not really."

"That's about to change." Kathi nodded vigorously in Laura's direction. "Tomorrow we are going to shop for something outrageously colorful for you."

"You know I hate to shop. . ." Laura began.

Kathi interrupted. "That's no excuse. It's just not healthy for a woman to hate shopping. It's positively unnatural. Shopping is not just the act of locating something to purchase, you know. It's so much more." With that curious statement, she captured her audience's undivided attention, so she continued on enthusiastically. "It's true. Shopping is therapy, a cure-all. Good for depression, insomnia, boredom, just about anything. Did I ever tell you about the woman I met who cured herself of an eating disorder by shopping?"

Laura giggled in spite of herself. Of all the outlandish statements Kathi had made over the years, and there had been plenty, this had to be the craziest.

Kathi was clearly stung by her friend's laughter, assuming correctly that it indicated her disbelief, and she opened her mouth in defense. "I mean it. . ."

The phone rang and Laura jumped to answer it, thankful for a diversion. It was Robert, calling to say that he and Graham would be picking them up at eight. Laura hung up the phone with a smile. She didn't even mind that Robert had made plans to escort her without her consent. After all, the four of them would be together. And tonight, if she got an opportunity to be alone with Graham, she would tell him she was a Christian. She could hardly wait to see the look on his face.

❧

"If you don't stop wiggling, I'm not going to be able to zip you up," Laura scolded her squirming roommate. Kathi stood motionless for a fraction of a second, and Laura successfully zipped her into her red-sequin dress. Just as Laura had predicted, the red dress enhanced Kathi's vivid coloring perfectly.

"You look lovely, Kathi. No doubt all eyes will be on you tonight," Laura pronounced affectionately.

Kathi whirled around, a broad smile on her face. "I'm not so sure. Take a peek in the mirror, Laura. Even in black," Kathi wrinkled her nose in distaste, "you look beautiful. In fact, tonight you look positively radiant." Kathi gave her a smug grin. "Must be the new man in your life."

Laura looked at herself in the mirror. There *was* a difference in her appearance tonight. And it wasn't her clothes. Her tea-length dress, a slim, black-lace sheath, was flattering with its scalloped hem and sleeves, but that wasn't what caught Laura's attention. It was her eyes. They seemed to glow with an inner light she had never noticed before.

She smiled at her reflection as she recognized the reason for the change. Kathi was right. It *was* the new man in her life. But not the man Kathi was referring to. Not a flesh and blood man. It was God. She knew instinctively it was the peace He gave her that put the sparkle in her eyes. One day, she would find the boldness to share that knowledge with Kathi, but for now, she just smiled, a deeply contented look that was not lost on her best friend.

A sharp rap on the door, promptly at eight, announced the arrival of their escorts. Both girls took a final peek in the full-length mirror before Laura moved to the door to open it. The sight that greeted her took her breath away.

Both men were clad in black tuxedos, with crisp, white, pleated shirts and black ties, but the similarity ended there. Robert looked nice, quite attractive actually, Laura conceded, but Graham gave new meaning to the word gorgeous.

He was the picture of elegance in his black tuxedo that hugged his broad shoulders and draped his muscular six-foot-four-inch frame flawlessly. The stark white of his shirt was the perfect backdrop for his golden tan and thick shock of dark, wavy hair that curled carelessly on his forehead and at the nape of his neck. When he raised his piercing gray eyes to meet hers and tossed her his customary broad smile, Laura's breath caught in her throat. He was so beautiful.

She could hear Robert speaking and reluctantly withdrew her gaze from Graham to acknowledge him.

"Laura!" Robert stepped forward, grasping her slim shoulders with his hands. "If possible, you look more lovely than ever." He smacked his lips appreciatively as he devoured her with his eyes. "I'll be the envy of every man there tonight."

Laura lowered her lashes shyly. Robert's effusive praise in front of Graham embarrassed her. "Thank you."

Kathi had joined them at the door, where she spun around to elicit Graham's approval of her dress. He chuckled warmly at the childlike overture. "Kathi, as always, you sparkle. I'll have to wield a bat to drive the men away."

Smiling with extreme satisfaction over his response, Kathi

tucked her petite arm through his muscular one, and the two of them led the way to dinner. Again a sharp jab drove into Laura's heart. They looked so handsome together, the perfect couple.

For the captain's reception, the dining room had been rearranged, with the tables forming a circle around a polished wooden dance floor. A stage had been erected for the orchestra which was playing a medley of contemporary tunes. Fresh flowers were in abundance, draping the stage and gracing each table, filling the air with their sweet fragrance, and the room was aglow with thousands of flickering candles.

The maitre d' directed them to their table. The Johnsons were already seated, and as usual, were so completely engrossed in one another, they scarcely noticed when the foursome arrived. Robert pulled out the chair for Laura to seat her, as Graham did for Kathi, and the two men took their places beside them.

Laura noted with concern that Graham's movements were laborious, as though he was still troubled with the stiffness he mentioned earlier. She thought she saw him wince as he lowered himself into the chair across from her.

She caught his eye and quirked her delicate eyebrow in question. He met her worried look with a melting smile that immediately dispelled all her fears. No one that felt rotten could look that good.

The captain of the ship, an attractive man Laura supposed to be in his early fifties, stood at the microphone on stage and proposed a toast to the crowd of elegantly clad passengers that filled the room. "To long and prosperous lives. May all your seas be smooth sailing," he intoned with a heavy European accent. The passengers cheered, clinked their glasses in toast, and drank to one another's good health.

As if on cue, waiters streamed into the dining room, carrying platters of delicious appetizers and salads. Immediately, a quiet settled over the room as the patrons delved into their meal.

"Tomorrow we'll be stopping in St. Thomas," Robert said between bites. "Anybody got any ideas about what we should do while we're there?"

"Laura and I have already made big plans to go shopping." Kathi answered enthusiastically, much to Laura's chagrin. "We'd love to have you handsome men accompany us, though." She raised her blue eyes coyly to meet Graham's.

Laura suppressed a groan. The only thing that she could imagine worse than shopping was to have to shop with an audience. A male audience. "Oh, Kathi, I'm certain the men aren't interested in stores. I'm sure they'd prefer to see the beaches on the island." *Which is what I would rather be doing,* she thought glumly.

"Nonsense, Laura," Robert said warmly, placing his hand on hers. "It would be a pleasure to shop with you. There are a few things I'd like to pick up while we are there."

Surprisingly, even Graham agreed. "Of course, we'll stay together. And if we have time after you ladies have hit the stores, we'll ride over to the beach. They'll have shuttle boats leaving the ship every hour, on the half hour. Suppose we catch the boat leaving the ship tomorrow at ten-thirty. That should leave us plenty of time to do both."

Laura could find no adequate response. The matter had been decided. Tomorrow, her first and probably only time on a lush, tropical island in the middle of the Caribbean, she would spend her day doing what she liked least, shopping.

With the arrival of coffee and dessert, the orchestra struck up a lively tune and many of the now-sated diners moved onto the dance floor.

Kathi leaned over and whispered something into Graham's ear. He nodded and after making some explanation that Laura couldn't hear over the music, the two rose from the table, and slipped hand-in-hand through the crowd and out into the hall. Laura's heart ached at the sight of them leaving. She hadn't even had the opportunity to tell Graham she'd become a Christian. She just had to tell him tonight.

Not wanting to be obvious, Laura waited a full fifteen minutes before she made her move. "Robert, if you'll excuse me, I think I'll run to the ladies' room." She excused herself and slipped past the tables and out into the hall where clusters of men and women, dressed in expensive finery, stood talking and laughing.

A glance to the right and left proved futile. *No sign of Kathi and Graham. Perhaps he escorted her to the ladies room,* she thought. *Maybe I can catch him there and tell him my good news.*

She turned left, thinking she had passed a ladies lounge as they had come in this evening. She had covered about one third of the corridor when she came to a dimly lit alcove. She stepped forward, moving into the entrance when she stopped short. Before her, hidden in the shadows, stood her roommate and chaperone, locked in an embrace. Kathi's arms were wrapped around Graham's neck and his face was within inches of hers, as if he were just about to kiss her.

A tiny gasp escaped as Laura whirled around and fled the scene. She moved swiftly down the hall, her heart pounding in her chest, with the intention of passing up the dining room and getting outside, to find a quiet place to think, but Robert's untimely appearance in the doorway scotched her plans.

"There you are," he said with a warm smile. "I know how likely you are to get lost without your map, so I thought I'd meet you by the door of the ladies' room." He studied her flushed face for a moment. "Is something wrong?"

"Wrong? No. . ., nothing's wrong," she stammered, while her heart screamed the reverse. *Everything is wrong! Graham and Kathi are madly in love, smooching in the hallway. What else could possibly go wrong?* She fidgeted anxiously with the bracelet at her wrist. "I'm ready to go back to the cabin if you don't mind. I'd like to get a good night's rest before our day in St. Thomas tomorrow."

"Sure," Robert nodded. "I'll be glad to take you up. Shouldn't we go find Father Graham and tell him where you are going?"

"NO!" Laura answered, a bit too fervently. "What I mean is, no, that won't be necessary. He won't worry." *He won't even notice,* she thought dismally.

In the span of a few seconds, Laura hatched a desperate plan. "And while we are on the subject of my chaperone, would you mind terribly if you and I went shopping alone tomorrow? We could catch the boat that leaves at nine-thirty, instead of waiting until ten-thirty to go with Graham and Kathi." *At least then I won't have to watch them together,* she added silently.

A broad grin swept Robert's face and a gleam shone in his dark eyes. "No, I don't mind. In fact, I think it's a wonderful idea. I'll meet you at the cabin at nine fifteen."

Laura caught the glint in his eyes, but there was no time to reconsider the wisdom of her plan. There was no other way out. "I'll be ready. Just don't knock. I wouldn't want to wake Kathi."

"It's a deal." Robert tucked her arm through his and led her upstairs to her cabin. Her thoughts were so jumbled, she was scarcely aware that they were moving, and before she knew it they stood before her cabin door.

"Thanks, Robert. Tonight was lovely," Laura murmured mechanically, with a blank glance up into his brown eyes. Before she could react, his arms pulled her into an embrace, and he kissed her soundly on the lips. She was too disheartened to care. She placed her hands on his chest, applying enough pressure to prevent him from pressing another moist kiss upon her, then turned to unlock her door with trembling hands.

"Good night Laura. Sweet dreams," Robert called after her retreating figure.

ta

Graham rounded the corner of the hall and paused for a moment, leaning against the wall to catch his breath. He looked up in time to see what he perceived to be a tender exchange between Laura and Robert. *Too late.* He'd gotten there too late. Although, from his present perspective, he wondered what he'd thought he could actually accomplish had he gotten there before them.

He'd caught a brief glimpse of Laura downstairs, while Kathi was trying, against his wishes, to massage his neck, but she'd run off before he could get her attention. Thinking perhaps she had gone back to the dining room, he'd dragged Kathi with him to find her. After finding the table empty, he had known she was gone. But where?

As a last resort, he left a disgruntled Kathi in her chair, and flew up the stairs, two at a time, to intercept the couple in the event they were on the way to Laura's door. He knew it was wrong to meddle, but the idea of Laura in Robert's arms was more than he could bear. Graham slumped against the wall, running his fingers through his wavy hair. He had been too late.

For a moment, he denied he had any other interest in Laura than her soul. He was simply watching out for his friend's daughter. But he knew better. It was time to face the facts. He loved her.

⁂

Laura closed the door to her cabin, and threw herself dejectedly onto her bed. Hot tears stung her eyes. Her heart literally ached. The picture of Kathi and Graham locked in an embrace burned torturously in her memory. She shouldn't be surprised, she told herself. She had known all along Kathi and Graham cared about each other. Why, Kathi had even said he was "the one." But to actually see them together, really together, was so painful.

Laura sobbed softly into her pillow. As always, her foray into relationships had left her with a broken heart. She had known that allowing herself to open up would make her vulnerable to hurt, but she had thought somehow this time would be different. She just wanted a friend.

Everything about Graham was different from any man she had ever known. He was kind, intelligent, and sensitive. He offered her friendship without expecting anything in return. Laura sighed as the irony of the situation struck home. Without trying, he had taken the one thing she had vowed never to give—her heart.

The truth was painfully clear. Laura was in love. After all these years, after all the protective insulation she had carefully wrapped herself in, she had finally fallen in love. With a man that would never return her love. With a man that was in love with her best friend.

"What's the matter with me?" she sobbed into the deafening silence of her room, "Will I always be alone?"

Suddenly, from somewhere deep within her, a tiny pinpoint of light glowed. A soothing voice, unlike the bitter one that usually harassed her, spoke with crystal clarity. *You are not alone, Laura.*

I'm here. When you hurt, I hurt. You're mine now. And you will never be alone again.

Laura sat up, wiping her tear-streaked face with the back of her hand. Although the words had not been spoken audibly, she knew she had heard them. And she knew Who had spoken them. She slipped off the bed and knelt penitently by the side.

"Dear God, what a mess I've made. I've fallen in love with my best friend's boyfriend, and now my heart feels like it's being twisted in two. I have made a date to spend the day with a man I care nothing for. And on top of all that, I had completely forgotten about You." Laura sniffled and wiped a stray tear.

"But You didn't forget about me, did You? It's just like Graham said. Christians don't face their problems alone." Laura's choked voice was barely a whisper. "Stay by me, God. I need you. I don't know how to face this problem alone."

twelve

Laura rolled over and looked at the alarm clock. Six A.M. The habit was so deeply ingrained, she automatically awoke at six for her run. But, this morning, instead of crawling out of the warm bed, she wrapped up in the covers and closed her eyes tightly, welcoming sleep.

This morning she would not run. She couldn't risk meeting Graham; she was afraid he would take one look at her and read the feelings she felt certain were emblazoned across her forehead. *I love Graham Kirkland, my best friend's boyfriend.* No, it would be best to put as much distance as she could between herself and him. It wouldn't be easy, not on a cruise ship in the middle of the Caribbean, but she'd do her best.

She slept fitfully for the next hour and a half. It was a relief to finally get up and ready for the day. She slipped into the bathroom and took a leisurely shower, feeling the warm water wash away the tensions of the night before.

She didn't have Graham, but she did have God, and between the two of them, they'd get through this. She held tightly to the words Graham had spoken. "Christianity is not a cure-all. We still have problems like everyone else. But we have victory in that we do not face the troubles alone."

Laura dressed in the darkened room. She pulled her gold-streaked tresses into a severe knot at the nape of her neck and slipped into a simple navy cotton dress.

She wrote a quick note to Kathi, who hadn't come in last night until past two A.M. and was still sound asleep. She explained that she and Robert had gone on ahead, and they would see them back on the ship that evening. She added the explanation that she wanted to surprise Kathi by shopping without her. *Who knows,* Laura thought with a weak smile, *maybe Kathi is right, maybe shopping is just the right therapy to cure a broken heart.*

She grabbed her handbag, and stepped silently into the hall to await Robert. She didn't have long to wait.

"Good morning, Laura. As always you are lovely beyond words," he greeted her with a smile. "Are you ready for a day of shopping?"

"I think so," she answered honestly, "although I can't say it's my favorite pastime."

Robert guided her down the hall into the waiting elevator. "St. Thomas may be just the experience you need to make you into a world class shopper. The shops are quaint, and the prices are extraordinary; everything in the islands is duty free you know."

Things could be completely free, and I still wouldn't like to shop, she thought rebelliously, but she turned a sweet smile to him.

They traveled down into the interior of the ship, six floors below the Olympic Deck to a small waiting room designated as the shore launch station. The room was already filled to capacity with excited passengers looking forward to a day on land, after several at sea. They were escorted out in groups of fifty, down a short flight of stairs, and through a heavy metal door. The passengers stepped out onto a platform just a few feet above sea level. Below them, an open boat waited to ferry them to the island.

Robert handed her down to the uniformed crewman and joined her; together they took a seat toward the front of the boat. Within minutes they were skimming across the surface of the sapphire blue water, the salty breeze buffeting them from all sides. Laura felt strangely exhilarated, a combination of relief from escaping without detection by Graham's watchful eye and the refreshing blast of sea air.

They pulled into the bustling harbor at St. Thomas, framed with a colorful raised backdrop of pristine, white buildings roofed in rich, red tiles, scattered amongst lush trees growing in green profusion on the hillside. The view was spectacular.

The crewman piloting the craft began issuing last-minute instructions over the public address system. He explained there would be a boat leaving the island every hour on the half hour to ferry them back to the *SS Scandinavia,* from this same dock. He also reported with a grin that the last boat would leave promptly at 5:30 P.M. and any passengers that were left on the island would remain there, permanently.

Finally, as the boat was being moored at the dock, the crewman offered basic directions to points of interest. He flashed a quick smile to the passengers that had risen to their feet, ready to disembark. "Don't forget, Cinderellas, the last coach leaves at five-thirty."

Robert took Laura's arm and led her down the wooden pier toward the shops. They crossed the street, dashing between the rushing cars, and walked under an arch suspended between two buildings into what Laura thought could best be described as an outdoor shopping mall.

White stucco buildings, replete with lacy wrought-iron balconies, lined a narrow, paved street that was closed to automobile traffic. Graceful awnings arching above shop windows fluttered in the slight breeze that wafted up Main Street. While Laura remained less than enthusiastic about shopping, she had to admit the setting was lovely and quaint.

"Where would you like to get started?" Robert asked.

"I would like to pick up a gift for my housekeeper, and my father too, so perhaps we should try jewelry first."

"Spoken like a true woman," Robert chuckled. "This looks like a popular spot," he said pointing to a shop on their right. "Let's try this one first."

The two of them followed the crowd into a large store. Rows of sparkling glass cases filled with fine jewelry and watches beckoned shoppers to review their finery.

Laura went right to work, moving briskly to a case displaying jewelry fashioned from pearls and coral. A pleasant clerk helped her select a coral bead necklace in a rich shade of rosy peach. "That will be perfect for Mrs. Reilly," Laura said with a satisfied smile.

Robert laughed. "It doesn't take you long to make up your mind, although I knew as soon as I met you that you were not the type of woman to be plagued with indecision." He patted her on the shoulder. "I like a woman that knows her own mind."

Laura chose not to respond, but a slight smile crept across her lips. She knew her quick decision was a product of her aversion to shopping, not her clear thinking. She just wanted to get out of the store as soon as possible.

"Let's find a watch for my dad," Laura said, already moving toward a case filled with Swiss watches. Robert trailed behind, watching her businesslike approach to shopping with amusement.

Five minutes later they left the store, Laura's purchases wrapped neatly and tucked into a colorful shopping bag emblazoned with the jewelry store logo, which she wore on her arm.

They strolled companionably along the street, enjoying the sights and sounds of the island. Robert paused in front of a tiny restaurant with an inviting flagstone patio. "Let's stop for something cold to drink."

Laura smiled her appreciation at his thoughtfulness. The slight breeze was not enough compensation for the scorching sun or the humidity in the air, and after walking only a few blocks, she felt hot and sticky. A cold drink sounded terrific.

The waiter seated them at a cozy, black, wrought iron table for two with a nice view of the street and the passing tourists. Robert ordered a fresh lemonade for both of them. Moments later, the waiter returned with two tall glasses of lemonade, each with one small cube of ice. Robert frowned into his drink.

"Is there a problem, sir?" the waiter asked. "You did not want the lemonade?"

"What I want is cold lemonade, with ice."

The waiter smiled patiently, as one would with an errant child. "You must be from the States? All those folks are crazy about ice." With that, he disappeared into the kitchen and returned momentarily, this time with a small cup in his hand. "For you, sir," he said, handing Robert the cup and walking away.

Robert looked into the cup with a puzzled expression marring his face. Laura peered over to see what was so interesting. Inside the cup were two small ice cubes. Laura began to laugh, and Robert, who appeared to be struggling to maintain his temper, joined in. "I guess this will have to do until we get back to the ship," he said with a laugh. Suddenly, he became serious. "Have I ever told you how desirable you are?"

Laura wasn't sure if he was trying to complement her or make a pass. She didn't want to hurt his feelings, but she wanted him to know she was not interested in romance.

"Have I told you what a wonderful friend you are for bringing me shopping this morning?" She placed special emphasis on the word "friend." It was actually true, she thought with amazement, this morning she did consider him a friend. After all, he had helped her escape.

Robert said nothing, choosing to smile at her instead, and the two of them sipped their lukewarm lemonade in comfortable silence.

"I've got to stop at a liquor store and pick up a few bottles of liquor before we go to the beach. Liquor here on the island is so cheap. My bar at home needs replenishing, and I told several friends I would bring them back a fifth," Robert said placing his empty glass on the table.

Laura frowned slightly. She had no intention of entering a liquor store. She knew that many adults indulged in an occasional drink, but she personally did not feel comfortable with alcoholic beverages. Her limited experience with people who had been drinking was all bad. "That's fine," she replied, "while you pick up your liquor, I'll find a dress shop and pick up a dress. Kathi will have my head, if I show up tonight without having purchased one."

Robert looked doubtful, as though he might insist upon accompanying her, so Laura added, "Just give me an hour, and I'll meet you back here. It'll save time."

Robert nodded his agreement. Fearing he might change his mind if she lingered, Laura rose to her feet, gathering her purse and shopping bag in her arms. "See you in an hour."

Laura paused just outside the restaurant, glancing around to get her bearings. She turned to the right, since they had come up to the restaurant from the left, and she did not recall having seen any dress shops in their travels.

The street was crowded with milling tourists. She found the jostling unpleasant, and moved quickly, trying to separate herself from the throng.

The first shop she stopped in was another jewelry store. She hadn't intended to purchase any more jewelry, but a heart-shaped locket in the window caught her eye. *It would be perfect for Kathi,* Laura thought with a grin. Within minutes, she reappeared from the store, a second shopping bag dangling from her arm, and a satisfied look on her face. "Now," she muttered to herself, "if only I can find a dress shop."

Another window caught her eye, this time one filled with every sort of music box imaginable. Laura couldn't resist a quick peek inside. After all, it would only take a minute to locate a brightly colored dress to please Kathi, and she still had three quarters of an hour left before she had to be back to meet Robert. Besides, she loved music boxes, especially the kind with animated figurines.

The shopkeeper, an elderly man with bushy, white eyebrows and parchment skin, recognized her at once as a kindred spirit, and he took great delight in showing her his most valued pieces. She was such an appreciative audience, that he even pulled out some of his prize antiques from a storeroom in the back. She oohed and aahed over them and listened with rapt attention as the merchant related the history of each piece.

The bell on the door of the shop tinkled, indicating the presence of another customer, and the shopkeeper politely excused himself to see to their needs. Laura glanced down at her watch and gasped; she'd been there for over half an hour. She had less than ten minutes to find a dress and get back to the restaurant to meet Robert.

"I'm sorry," she called to the owner, "it's been so interesting that I hate to leave, but I see I have stayed too long. I've got to meet my traveling companion in just a few minutes." She sighed wistfully. "Maybe if we have time, I'll get back before the ship sails this evening."

"It was my pleasure to spend the morning with so lovely a young lady." He bowed gallantly, and walked her to the door. "I hope I will see you again."

Laura left the store and continued rapidly up the street in search of a dress shop. She had covered the block when she noticed a short side street to her left, with several stores opening onto it. She stepped in, and to her relief, the very first window was decorated with mannequins modeling island fashions.

A slender woman met her at the door. "May I help you find something?"

"Please, I am looking for a sundress. Something with a lot of color, if you have it," Laura replied, as her eyes darted around the store looking for something suitable.

"A woman with coloring such as yours would be lovely in pink. Let me see if I can find you something." The sales clerk moved toward the rack of dresses and began methodically sifting through them. "Aha! What about something like this?"

Laura's time was quickly running out. "That's perfect. I'll take it."

"But first you must try it on. It would be a shame to purchase a dress you can not wear." The woman herded a reluctant Laura toward the dressing room as she spoke. "It will only take a minute."

Laura slipped off her navy dress in record time and pulled the sundress over her head. A quick check in the mirror indicated the fit was fine; the dress would be perfect. Even Kathi would be satisfied. She dressed again in her own clothes and carried the sundress to the register to pay for it. While the sales clerk was ringing up her purchase, a large group of noisy women, chattering in a language Laura did not recognize, burst into the tiny store.

"The shop is so small, there is not room for us all to breathe." The clerk shook her head in disgust. "You will never get past them."

It was true; the women, most of them of significant girth, now crowding into the front of the store effectively blocked her passage back outside. Laura glanced at her watch. She was already several minutes overdue. "I'm in an awful hurry, do you have another door that leads outside?"

"Yes, the back door opens on to an alley that runs behind the stores. You could go to the end of the alley and take a left through the passageway leading to Main Street. It's not very clean back there, but it'll work if you're in a hurry. It's only a couple of blocks, and you wouldn't have to wade through the crowds."

Laura thanked her for her help, gathered her bundles in her arms, and stepped through the back of the shop, out into the alley.

The alley, a dark and narrow corridor flanked on both sides by concrete walls, was used for depositing garbage rather than for accommodating shoppers. In the heat of the day, the cans of refuse had soured, and Laura could scarcely breathe.

Stacks of cans and boxes leaning against the graffiti-covered walls cast eerie shadows, and Laura felt suddenly afraid. She tried to dispel the unpleasant feeling that she was being watched.

"Dear God," she prayed silently, "help me."

A scraggly cat jumped into her path, frightening her half out of her wits and causing her to drop her packages to the ground.

"It's just a poor kitty," she whispered to herself, as she bent to retrieve the scattered packages. The heat in the alley was stifling and tiny beads of perspiration formed on Laura's upper lip. She walked quickly, her parcels clutched to her chest, glancing nervously from side to side. To her relief, she could see a shaft of light up ahead. The passageway to Main Street. She'd made it.

About fifteen feet in front of her, between her and the passageway, a man suddenly stepped out from the shadows, his face obscured in the dim light. He stood in the middle of the alley, facing her, as though he were waiting for her.

"Hello? Who's there? What do you want?" Laura spoke in a timorous voice she scarcely recognized as her own.

The man stepped forward, with his hand outstretched toward her. He said nothing.

Laura stopped, fear making her feet like lead. Something was wrong here. "I said, what do you want?"

The man moved slightly, and light from the passageway poured in behind him, reflecting off the object he held in his hand. It was a knife. A switchblade. He waved it menacingly. "I want your packages and your purse, little lady. Put the bags on the ground!" he demanded with a thick accent.

Without hesitation, Laura dropped the bags. She could always buy more gifts. Her mind was racing. Should she scream? Would anyone even hear her, or would she just incense the man, causing him to react violently? Fear that only a frightened croak would come forth kept her silent.

She deliberated whether or not she should try to run back to the dress shop. If she could outrun him, she might find safety there. She remembered the heavy steel door had no knob on the outside. While she pounded on the door to be heard, her assailant would most likely be cutting her to bits. As was her habit when nervous, she twisted the diamond bracelet at her wrist, unaware that the light danced off the brilliant gems.

"I'll take that too," he growled, motioning toward her wrist. He took a slow step toward her, the switchblade clutched in the palm of his hand, the sharp blade directed toward her.

This time Laura hesitated. The bracelet was her mother's graduation gift to her. It was irreplaceable. He seemed to sense her defiance, and he took another slow, deliberate step forward, calculating his next move. By now she could see his face; he was unshaven, his dark features twisted with malice.

Terror filled her. Her legs were frozen in place. There was no way out. She was going to die.

From behind her, she could hear footsteps stealthily approaching. Her assailant's accomplice. Laura closed her eyes in resignation.

"Drop it. NOW!" A thunderous voice commanded.

Laura's heart ceased to beat. The combination of sweltering heat and palpable fear pushed her beyond her endurance, and she reacted as any red-blooded woman would under the circumstances. She fainted.

thirteen

Laura's eyes fluttered open. Struggling to focus, she searched the unfamiliar surroundings for a clue as to where she was. She was lying on a small cot in a brightly lit room that was stacked to the ceiling with boxes. What was she doing here she wondered. And where was here?

Her memory flooded back in a chilling wave. She remembered she had been out in the alley, and there had been a man with a knife, and. . .Laura pushed herself to an upright position. Her mind was reeling. Had he stabbed her? Was she dead? Surely this messy little room wasn't heaven. She was no Bible scholar, but somewhere she had heard of streets paved in gold. She closed her eyes for a moment, and opened them again, hoping to clear her befuddled mind.

A slight movement in the doorway snared her attention, and she looked over, into the fathomless gray eyes of Graham Kirkland. She lay back, a broad smile on her face. Maybe this was heaven after all.

"You're awake." Graham rasped, his deep voice clouded with an emotion that Laura could not name. With two long strides, he was sitting beside her on the cot, holding her in his arms. His muscular arms crushed her against his chest so tightly that it was difficult for Laura to draw a full breath. But she wasn't complaining. It felt wonderful.

"Laura, what in the world were you doing back there?" Graham shuddered and pulled her even more tightly to him. "You could have been killed."

She rested against his broad chest, considering the truth of his statement. She realized how foolish she had been. An interesting thought struck her. "It's funny, you know, I thought I was going to die, and while I was terribly frightened of the pain of being

111

stabbed, I wasn't really afraid of death." Laura pulled back slightly, raising her soft brown eyes to his. "I'm a Christian now, Graham," she whispered shyly. "I accepted Jesus as my Savior, so now I don't have to fear death. I have eternal life."

With a strangled groan, Graham pulled her back into his protective embrace. "Sweet Laura, that doesn't mean we Christians should go around courting death." He sighed deeply, and drew her back to look into her face. "I'm very glad to hear you are a Christian now." His gray eyes locked with hers. "Your father and I have been praying for you for a very long time . . ." he stopped, unable to continue, as deep emotion constricted his throat.

A woman Laura recognized as the sales clerk from the dress shop entered the room, and handed her a styrofoam cup. "Here, honey, drink this; it'll make you feel better."

Laura obediently took a sip, then lowered the cup, a smile stealing across her lips. It was water, lukewarm.

"I feel so awful about what happened out there. I never dreamed there would be anyone in the alley to bother you." The clerk's dark eyes grew wide. "Why, if your man hadn't come along, you could be. . . ." She couldn't make herself finish the statement. "It's all my fault."

Laura shook her head. "It wasn't all your fault. I'm afraid I let the time get away from me." She turned to Graham in a sudden panic. "Oh, no. What about Robert? I was supposed to meet him at the restaurant."

Graham's heart sank at the mention of Robert. He had enjoyed holding her in his arms, pretending she cared for him. "I sent him and Kathi on to the beach," he said, and seeing her bewildered expression, he explained further, "I saw him sitting out on a restaurant patio, so I stopped to ask him where you were. When he told me you were off shopping, I asked him to take Kathi on to the beach, and told him you and I would join them there." *What an understatement,* he thought, a grin tugging at the corner of his mouth.

Actually, by the time he had run into Robert at the restaurant that morning he was already in a black mood. After witnessing the kiss Robert and Laura had exchanged the night before, and then finding that the two of them went on to the island without him that morning, Graham was furious. When he saw Robert sitting there, his temper snapped.

Graham stormed over to him, Kathi following helplessly in his wake, and slammed his fists down on the table. "What in the world were you thinking, going off this morning without Kathi and me? Didn't I make it clear we would all come to the island together?"

Robert flushed crimson and stammered his reply, "I'm, I'm sorry, Graham. I didn't think you'd mind. After all, it was Laura's idea."

That simple declaration cut deeply. It had been Laura's idea to leave him behind. It seemed that at every opportunity, she found a way for the two of them to be alone, away from Graham. The only gratification he could draw from the confrontation was the knowledge that he had thoroughly intimidated Robert. The pleasure, however, was short lived.

"Where is she now?" Graham asked, somewhat mollified.

Robert drew a deep breath, as if he were fearful to answer the question. He stared into his hands as he spoke, "She went shopping for a dress. She insisted upon going alone." He glanced nervously toward Graham. "She said she'd be back in an hour, although she's a bit late." He tried to sound casual. "She must have found a great sale somewhere, and forgot the time. Typical woman."

Warning bells went off in Graham's head. Just that morning, Kathi had mentioned Laura loathed shopping. Why would someone who hated shopping, take any longer than necessary to find what they needed?

The first thought that crossed his mind was that she was lost. Even within the confines of the ship, she had managed to wander off in the wrong direction several times.

Graham leaned toward Robert, both hands braced on the tabletop. "How could you have let her go alone?" he growled ominously. "She gets lost on her way to the ladies' room." He stopped.

This conversation was wasting valuable time. With barely suppressed anger he bit out, "Take Kathi with you to the beach. Stay with her, for heaven's sake. I'll find Laura and meet you there. If we are detained, we'll all meet back on the ship. Do you understand?"

Before dashing off in search of her, he asked Robert for a description of what Laura was wearing and if he had seen which way Laura had gone. From there, it had been relatively easy to find her. He walked several blocks in the direction Robert had indicated when he came upon an elderly gentlemen standing in the doorway of a shop, surveying the crowded street.

By what Graham considered at the time to be a remarkable coincidence, and which he now recognized as the hand of God, Graham stopped to ask the man if he had seen a tall, slender blond in a navy dress that morning. He knew it was like searching for a needle in a haystack, and yet, to his astonishment, the man had indeed seen her and had even seen her go into a dress shop farther down the street.

The old gentlemen delayed Graham slightly, while he went into his shop, and came out carrying a package he said belonged to the lovely young lady. Graham thanked him and hurried on to the dress shop.

The small store was filled to capacity with a group of rotund shoppers. Had it not been for his superior height, the clerk would not have noticed him at all. Once they were able to speak, he described Laura, and the clerk replied with a smile that yes, she had been there and had left only minutes before, by way of the alley.

Satisfied he had located her before any harm had come to her, he took his time, walking leisurely through the back of the store and out into the alley. He was deliberating whether or not he should reprimand her for leaving him behind.

Within seconds after his eyes adjusted to the dim light in the alley, he spotted her several yards up ahead, engaged in a conversation with someone. There was no indication she was in danger, and yet, Graham felt compelled to remain out of sight as he approached her. Again, in retrospect, he was able to see clearly it was the hand of God preventing him from rushing to her, which could possibly have driven her attacker to harm her.

Graham shuddered involuntarily. The thought that harm would come to Laura was too horrible to contemplate. Unconsciously, he pulled her back into the shelter of his embrace.

He almost smiled as he recalled his reaction to the armed man. When he saw the knife pointed at Laura, he went berserk, charging forward, shouting something, he couldn't remember what, to attempt to frighten the man away.

Miraculously, it had worked. The man fled down the alley and through a passage on the left. He chuckled softly. His reaction must have looked like an enraged mother bear protecting her cubs.

Absently, he stroked her honey-gold hair. Laura stirred slightly in his arms, nestling closely against his chest, her slender arms stealing around his waist. He did want to protect her. Always.

Graham's thoughts shifted to Laura's new-found faith and conversion. He was truly delighted that she had found salvation, but the happiness was tempered with a sense of loss. It seemed his purpose in being with Laura was fulfilled. She was now a child of God. It was time to withdraw his attentions from her, to relinquish her to the man she loved.

Graham sighed with resignation. Ever so gently, he released her and stood up, needing to separate himself further from her physically before he went against his best intentions and swept her into his embrace again.

Two uniformed police officers walked into the tiny room. "Ma'am," the shorter of the two spoke, "we'd like to ask you some questions, if you are feeling up to it."

Laura nodded, running a hand through her disheveled hair. She cast a worried look toward Graham who now stood in the corner, her eyes pleading with him to stay. He nodded his affirmation and flashed her an encouraging smile.

The officers, who were summoned by the shopkeeper, stayed more than an hour, asking Laura to describe the assailant, and to repeat anything he said to her. She complied, telling and retelling the story until the police were satisfied.

"Thank you, ma'am, for your cooperation," the first officer spoke, snapping his notepad shut. "You are a lucky little lady that your friend here showed up when he did. We have had trouble with this sort of thing before: burglars wait out in the alley for the shopkeepers to open their back doors and throw out their trash. The burglar knocks them over their heads, or worse, and then. . ."

The officer noticed the color draining from Laura's face and decided to drop the subject. He slipped the pad into his back pocket. "You can be sure we'll do everything we can to capture the man. Thank you again for your help."

Both officers shook her hand, then Graham's hand, and exited out the back door in search of clues.

"Laura, what do you want to do now?" Graham asked, carefully maintaining a safe distance between them. "Do you still want to go to the beach, or should I take you back to the ship?"

What I truly want is for you to hold me close again, she thought. It had been wonderful to be held within the protective confines of his strong arms. It had felt so right. Leaning against the broad expanse of his chest, she had pretended he held her tenderly because he returned her love. She had to restrain herself from clutching him when he had pulled away.

Realization dawned on her as to what had precipitated him withdrawing his arms that had cradled her so gently. *I put my arms around him,* she thought with horror. *I actually hugged him. He was probably afraid that I was taking his ministrations the wrong way, when he's in love with Kathi.*

A rosy blush stole across her face. *Graham is Kathi's boyfriend. He tried to offer me comfort, as any friend would do, and I've tried to make it into something romantic.* She colored more brightly. *No wonder he moved away. He was probably afraid I'd tackle him.*

Laura's voice was barely a whisper. "Would you mind terribly if we just went back to the ship. I don't really feel like going to the beach anymore."

Graham nodded in understanding. "Stay there for a minute,

while I collect all your things, and then we'll head back to the docks." He walked out of the room.

Laura slumped back against the cot in dismay. *What am I going to do? Graham is Kathi's.* Pretending his attention was anything more than friendship was disloyal to two people she loved very much. Who happened to be in love with each other.

I've got to get over him, she thought desperately. She closed her eyes, formulating a plan. *I know I can't stand to see Graham and Kathi together—it's too painful, and apparently I can't see Graham by himself without making a fool of myself. I just can't be with him any more. It's that simple.* She sat up with a new determination.

Today was Wednesday and the ship docked in Miami on Sunday. *Surely, I can stay away from him for that long.* A sad twinge plucked at her heart. She liked being with Graham. He was a wonderful friend. She would miss talking with him. She would miss gazing into his incredible eyes. But it would be for the best.

The two of them walked back to the dock through the crowded streets in silence, each wrestling with the feelings they sought to override. The boat was already waiting and partially loaded when they arrived, and within minutes they were sailing over the rolling waves.

Graham maintained his distance, careful that not even his shoulder should bump hers. Laura sat rigidly in her seat, purposefully avoiding any contact with him. To an outside observer they looked more like mannequins than humans. The awkward silence was deafening.

The ferry finally reached the *SS Scandinavia* and the passengers began to disembark. Laura stood up to exit when the boat lurched suddenly, throwing her into Graham's arms. A current surged through them at the contact. Both reacted immediately. Graham pulled back his arms that had caught her as though he had been burned and stared intently at the floor. Laura planted both feet firmly on the bottom of the boat to steady herself and nervously looked away, afraid to meet Graham's eyes.

The crewman helping the passengers off the boat had witnessed the episode and now stared with barely concealed amusement at the nervous pair. "When you two shrinking violets are ready, I'll let you off and go back to pick up another load," he teased.

Both jumped as though they had been stung, scrambling off the boat and onto the dock without looking back, even as the crewman's laughter followed them on the breeze.

Once inside the shore launch station, Graham's broad shoulders began to shake with suppressed mirth. Laura saw the merry smile on his face, and she, too, began to giggle. Somehow, the teasing jibe had successfully broken the wall of silence separating them. Graham extended his arm to Laura with exaggerated gallantry, and she accepted the gesture with a curtsy, allowing him to escort her to her cabin. The conversation flowed easily now, the two friends enjoying the companionship of one another.

At the door of the cabin, Laura paused. "Thank you again for rescuing me. I shudder to think what would have happened if you hadn't arrived when you did." Her dancing brown eyes suddenly became solemn.

Graham restrained the arms that threatened to embrace her, shoving his hands deeply into his pockets. "You have God to thank for the rescue, actually. In spite of what the officer said, I don't believe it was luck that caused me to arrive in time. I believe without a shadow of a doubt that God led me to you. It was just too easy to be coincidence."

Laura nodded. "I remember whispering a prayer in the alley." She turned a wide-eyed look toward Graham. "Isn't it amazing that He was listening?" Her voice reflected the awe that she felt. "I mean, that the Creator of the universe cares about me."

Graham smiled tenderly. "That reminds me. A new Christian needs to read the Bible. It's a terrific way to get to know your heavenly Father and to find out just how much He does care about you." He pulled a small leather volume from the back pocket of his jeans and placed it in her hands. "Use mine until we can get you one of your own."

Laura ran her hand over the worn book, an impish grin on her face.

"What's so funny?" Graham queried suspiciously.

Laura laughed brightly. "Kathi and I were right all along. You *are* a Bible-toting holy roller! The Bible is just much smaller than I imagined." *And the holy roller is much more wonderful than I imagined,* she wanted to add.

Graham chuckled deeply, flashing her his dazzling white smile. Her smitten heart skipped a beat.

She became serious, remembering her earlier resolution to avoid Graham's company. "I don't think I'll make it to dinner tonight. I'm exhausted from all the excitement today," she improvised.

Graham's gray eyes mirrored his concern. "Bless your heart. Go lie down. You'll need to rest up for our stop in San Juan tomorrow."

"I won't be going in to San Juan, either," Laura added hastily. "I, uh, I need to, uh, get my costume ready for the party tomorrow night."

Graham was not convinced of the sincerity of her response. He suspected she was afraid today's mishap might be repeated on the island tomorrow. "You don't have to worry about any more robbery attempts, Laura. I'll stay with you."

That's just what I'm afraid of, she thought. "No really, I'm not afraid of boogey men," she answered with forced levity. "I just need the time to put together a costume for the party." She avoided his piercing gaze. "You and Kathi and Robert go on without me, and I'll expect a full report when you return in the afternoon."

"Nonsense, if you stay, then I'll stay on board with you."

"Absolutely not!" Laura panicked. "What I mean is, Kathi will need you to escort her. Besides, I'll be busy all day. After I finish my costume, I'm looking forward to attending some lectures that sounded interesting." She could see he was wavering. "Really, Graham, I insist."

In the fear that continued discussion would be to her disadvantage, she decided to terminate it and go in. Turning her back to Graham, she unlocked the door and stepped inside. "Thanks again for everything."

As Graham handed her the packages he had been carrying for

her, his hand accidentally brushed against hers. Again, a current of electricity surged through them at the contact. Graham backed nervously into the hallway. "Call me if you need anything."

Laura nodded shyly, "See you tomorrow."

Once inside the cabin, Laura dropped the packages on the bed and glanced at the travel clock. *Only 2:15. What a day!*

She studied her reflection in the mirror on the closet door with dismay. At least a third of her hair had escaped from the knot, and straggled around her shoulders. Her navy dress was rumpled and dirty. She even had a streak of dirt on her cheek. Good thing she wasn't trying to impress Graham, she thought wryly. In the few days they had been together, he had seen her at her absolute worst.

Laura's stomach growled fiercely reminding her that on top of everything else, she was hungry as a bear. She hadn't had any breakfast, nor any lunch. She couldn't risk going down to the restaurant, Graham might be there and see her. She frowned. She hadn't considered that. This seclusion thing might be a problem after all. She decided to call the room steward and ask him to bring a salad to the room.

While waiting for lunch, she opened her packages to inspect the day's purchases. She hung the new sundress in her closet, noting with pleasure that the bright color of the dress was a cheerful addition to the somber navies and blacks. The watch and necklace were tucked into her luggage for safekeeping, and she placed the locket on Kathi's pillow for her to discover when she returned. Laura smiled in anticipation of Kathi's reaction.

Finally, Laura came to a bag she did not recognize. Thinking perhaps it was Graham's, she set it aside to return to him later. Her eyes were drawn back to the package as if it were a magnet. Curiosity got the best of her, and she determined a tiny peek wouldn't matter.

Inside the bag was a white cardboard box with a note attached. The note read:

I hope you don't mind accepting a gift from an old

*man. This has always been a special favorite of mine,
and so I want you to have it.*

Regards,
William Stern

Now Laura's curiosity was truly piqued. Who was William Stern?

She lifted the lid of the box and gasped. Inside, nestled in a bed of tissue paper was a beautiful, bone-china music box. Now she knew. William Stern was the shopkeeper she'd met earlier. Mr. Stern had sent her a gift.

Laura gently removed the music box from its wrapping. It was a lovely tranquil landscape, painted in muted pastels. Two tiny trees with leaves of red and gold flanked a narrow stream that curved through a pale-green meadow. It was so delicate, each minute detail perfectly proportioned, reflecting expert craftsmanship.

Laura turned the key at the bottom. A soft lullaby played while the scene revolved on its base. Laura was entranced. How kind of Mr. Stern to think of her! An inscription on the base caught her eye. *John 14:27.* She wasn't certain, but she thought that might be a reference to a Bible verse.

She retrieved Graham's Bible from the nightstand and looked for John 14:27. It was slow going, but she finally located the verse and what she read amazed her. "Peace I leave with you; my peace I give you. I do not give to you as the world gives. Do not let your hearts be troubled and do not be afraid."

Tears trickled down her cheeks. Those timely words spoke to her heart as though God Himself whispered them in her ear. The God she had consciously been avoiding all these years cared for her, and He wanted to be absolutely certain she knew. God cared, and He had something for her. It was peace. First, Graham had mentioned it, then Mr. Stern's generous gift had confirmed it.

She had already experienced in small measure the peace described here. The turmoil with which she had boarded the ship on Sunday was gone; in its place, a quiet lingered, and Laura knew it to be the peace of God.

Her brush with death this morning had been a second taste of the peace of God. Just as she had related to Graham, even the threat of death was no longer frightening. She had the assurance of eternal life.

She caressed the delicate piece and laid it lovingly on the table beside her. What a perfect reminder of God's promise of peace! She would treasure it always.

Later that afternoon, after she had eaten and showered, Laura turned on the music box again, and reread the Bible verse. "Peace I leave with you; my peace I give you. I do not give to you as the world gives. Do not let your hearts be troubled and do not be afraid." That same peace washed over her in a soothing wave and she closed her eyes in slumber.

❧

A noise outside the room awakened Laura. She blinked her sleep-heavy eyes, struggling to clear her groggy mind. She was lying on top of her bed, dressed in her bathrobe, in the now-darkened cabin. She glanced toward the clock on the nightstand: *10:35 P.M. I must have dozed off,* she thought.

Laura could hear Kathi's voice in the hall, and heard her put the key in the lock. Quickly, she slipped under the covers and pulled the blanket up under her chin, feigning sleep. The door swung open, and Laura could hear their voices more clearly.

"Is she asleep?" Graham spoke in a whisper.

Kathi studied the motionless form in the bed. "Yes."

"Does she look all right? I mean, you know, peaceful?"

Kathi giggled. "I think it would be all right if you took a quick peek."

Laura could hear him approach the bed, and through nearly closed lids could see his shadow fall across her face. His hand gently brushed aside a strand of hair that fell across her cheek.

"Bless her heart, she's had a rough day."

Graham moved toward the door where Kathi whispered something to him that Laura could not make out. The door opened again, then closed, and all was quiet once more. Laura waited, listening for the sound of Kathi moving within the room. Silence. Laura raised a tentative lid. No Kathi. Laura's heart sank. They'd gone back out.

A picture of Kathi in Graham's arms formed in her mind. It hurt to think of them together. Her gaze was drawn to the music box on the night table beside her. The luminous dial of the travel clock glowed behind it, outlining the tiny landscape in a greenish glow.

Peace. She had experienced God's peace, but somehow, in matters of love, it eluded her. Her heart ached. It hurt so terribly to love someone that loved someone else. She drew a shaky breath. This must be what Graham had been talking about when he'd said that Christians had problems like everyone else. Laura closed her eyes. "Dear God, I guess Christians aren't exempt from broken hearts. Thank You that You are in it with me. Help me find the victory. Amen."

fourteen

Laura slipped into the back of the crowded conference room and dropped into a vacant chair. She surveyed the gray-haired crowd with bewilderment. She recognized many of the wrinkled faces from the lecture she had attended previously. How in the world did all these old gals beat her to the room? She smiled as she realized that they probably hadn't taken a wrong turn at the boiler room as Laura had, and ended up at the far end of the ship. *Next time,* she decided with a grin, *I'll remember to take my map with me.*

A lovely woman that Laura guessed to be in her early thirties moved to the front of the room. She was dressed in a white lab coat and white hose and shoes to match. "Welcome, ladies," she began, in an overly cheery voice. "This morning I'd like to talk to you about the exciting world of fragrances, and how you can use them to allure members of the opposite sex."

The female audience, a majority of them over 70, giggled delightedly. Laura suppressed a groan and sank lower into her chair. *What have I gotten myself into now?*

After having spent the last hour in a deadly dull ice carving demonstration, Laura was a bit restless. She'd give anything to be up on the jogging trail, running out her frustrations in the sea breeze. Instead, she would be spending the next hour listening to a lecture on perfumes.

No point in complaining, she told herself. After all, it was her fault. She had told everyone she wanted to attend lectures instead of going ashore, and had even promised to give them a full report, so now she had to stay.

Laura closed her eyes and replayed the last few hours over in her mind. It had all started early this morning with Robert's frantic call. "Laura, I've been so worried about you. I can't believe that you were almost robbed yesterday. I feel so responsible. I should never have let you go off alone."

"Nonsense," Laura replied lightly. "I was foolish to take a short-cut through a deserted alley. Besides, all's well that ends well, and I'm fine."

Robert sighed heavily. "I'm so glad. I've been worried sick. I'd have called last night, but Father Graham insisted you were exhausted and couldn't be disturbed."

"Thank you for your concern, but I promise I'm fine."

"Feeling well enough to go into San Juan with me this morning?" He sounded so hopeful.

"I can't, Robert. I've made all sorts of plans aboard the ship today," she replied smoothly.

"Oh, I see. Well, what about dinner tonight?"

Laura felt terrible about refusing him, but she had to follow through with her plan. *Avoid Graham Kirkland at all costs.* "I won't be able to do that either. I've uh, got some things to do to get ready for the costume party." She paused, then added, "But I'll see you at the party."

Robert sounded disappointed as they hung up, making Laura feel guilty, but she knew that she must avoid Kathi and Graham. Until she got her feelings for Graham under control, she couldn't risk seeing them together. It was too painful.

As soon as she hung up with Robert, Kathi, who had been awakened by the ringing phone, threw her arms around Laura and demanded to hear all about her "brush with death." She listened to Laura recount the story with wide-eyed amazement.

"Oh, Laura, it was so horrible. No wonder you don't want to go into San Juan." Kathi patted her arm reassuringly. "When Graham told me you wanted to stay on board today to work on your costume, I knew that it was just an excuse you'd made up because you were scared. After all, I know your costume for tonight is finished. I helped you make it."

Laura swallowed hard. She was trapped. She'd told so many lies that she was tangled in their web. Before she had a chance to speak, Kathi, who seemed to sense her discomfort, spoke again.

"Don't worry; your secret is safe with me. I won't tell. In fact, I'll stay on board with you. You and I haven't spent much time together this week. We can go see that ice carving demonstration I was reading about."

"No!" Laura answered with a start. If Kathi didn't go ashore, then Graham wouldn't go ashore. "You're right, Kathi," she confessed, "it was an excuse. My costume is finished. Actually, I just wanted the day to myself so I could do some serious thinking."

That part was true, Laura consoled herself. She did need to do some thinking. About how to get herself out of the mess she'd made. It was time to come clean about her feelings for Robert. She didn't feel right about all the lies, not even for a good cause.

She'd wait until tonight, after everyone had returned from their day on the island, and then she'd confess to Kathi that she had mislead her into believing she cared for Robert. By now, Graham and Kathi's feelings for each other should be sufficiently strong, and Kathi wouldn't need her to spend time with Robert. And Graham would see that Laura was able to entertain herself quite nicely all alone, so he wouldn't feel responsible for her any more. It was all so simple, and yet it filled her with dread. It was difficult to admit to lying, especially to one's best friend. Laura didn't know how to begin, but she must.

"Serious thinking? About anyone I know?" A wide grin spread across Kathi's face.

"Yes, it's Robert," Laura replied absently, too caught up in her thoughts to see the erroneous conclusion that Kathi had drawn.

"Is there something you'd like to tell me?"

"Yes, it's something you and I need to talk about, but I'd like a little more time before I spring it on you."

"How exciting!" Kathi clapped her hands together with glee. "And I've got something I'd like to talk to you about." She leaned toward Laura and whispered conspiratorially, "It's about Graham."

Laura's heart sank. She wasn't so sure she wanted to hear.

"Oh, I almost forgot. I love my locket!" Kathi embraced her again. "You are the most thoughtful, wonderful friend in the world." She pulled back and studied Laura at arm's length. "I truly don't deserve you." She nodded solemnly as her blue eyes bored into Laura's.

Laura looked away, ashamed of what Kathi might find reflected in her eyes. *She's right,* Laura thought dismally; *she doesn't deserve a friend like me. I'm a traitor. A friend who's in love with her fiancé. A friend who practically threw herself at her best friend's future husband.* She hung her head in shame.

Kathi gave her a quick peck on the cheek, and bounded across the room toward the bathroom. "I've got to hurry. Graham will be here any minute, and I'm not dressed."

"You're awfully cheerful for someone who didn't get to bed until after two in the morning." Laura wished she hadn't said it the minute the words dropped from her lips.

Kathi called through the open door. "I guess you don't need as much sleep when you're in love."

Laura was thankful that Kathi couldn't see the tears that burned in her eyes, begging to be shed. No matter how hard she tried not to, she loved Graham. And Graham loved Kathi. Her heart felt as though it were being wrenched in two, the stabbing pain driving deeply through her chest. *How long is it going to hurt like this?* Where was the victory in suffering?

Kathi reappeared from the bathroom, dressed in a bright green sundress with a matching green scarf tying back her dark curls. "No sign of Graham yet?"

Laura jumped nervously off the bed. "Nope. Guess I'll take a quick shower before breakfast." She hurried past Kathi toward the bathroom and called over her shoulder, "Have a great day!"

"Don't you want to say hi to Graham? He'll want to see you to be sure you're all right after yesterday."

"No, uh, I'm really in a hurry," Laura faltered. "Tell him I'm just fine." She ducked into the bathroom and closed the door, leaving Kathi to face him alone.

❧

Laura opened her eyes. The lecturer was winding up the first segment of her speech. "Let's take a short break, ladies, and when we come back, I'll have some perfumes here for you to sample."

The room was buzzing with excited chatter. Laura seized the opportunity to escape and edged out of the room without being noticed.

She raced back to her cabin, changed into her running clothes and was out on the jogging deck in a matter of minutes. The breeze whipped across her face and through her braided hair in its customary greeting, and she breathed deeply. In spite of her worries, out here in the sea air, she felt free.

The jogging deck was more crowded than it was at 6 A.M., and Laura found herself weaving around the many runners that loped along at a more leisurely pace. She ran with abandon today, her feet flying along the polished planks. Strenuous exercise proved to be the perfect tonic, albeit temporary, for a broken heart.

fifteen

"Seems quiet without the ladies here tonight," Robert took a third stab at polite conversation with the grim-faced man across from him. "I guess they want to surprise us at the party with their costumes."

Graham shrugged. He was in no mood for conversation, especially not with Robert. He continued to toy with the food on his plate.

Robert gulped his scotch and water, wracking his brain for a subject Graham might be interested in. His thinking was somewhat muddled by the third, or was it the fourth, drink he'd imbibed since he'd arrived at dinner. He hadn't missed Graham's raised eyebrow when he had ordered the last drink, but he blamed Graham for the fact he was drinking at all. After being impaled by his fierce stare all night, Robert's nerves were shot. He had hoped a drink or two would help him say what he wanted to say.

"You know, Graham, there's something I'd like to talk to you about," Robert began after another fortifying gulp.

Graham leveled a steely look at him.

"It's about Laura. I guess you know I am fond of her," he paused, looking toward Graham in the hopes he would say something to alleviate Robert's discomfort.

Graham remained stone-faced and silent.

"Yes, well, anyway," Robert continued uneasily, "I felt perhaps I should talk with you first, seeing as how you are such a close friend of hers, rather like a brother, I'd say. Would you say that's a fair summation of your relationship?"

Graham winced imperceptibly, but nodded his assent.

Robert was visibly relieved to receive some sort of response from his companion. He took another long draught of his scotch. "Perhaps you could help me with a problem I'm having. You see,

I'm not quite sure how to approach Laura. She's a bit of a mystery to me."

Graham said nothing, but leaned back in his chair with his arms folded over his chest and continued to stare unblinking at Robert.

Robert emptied his glass in a swallow and signaled the waiter for another refill. "Do you see my dilemma?" Still no response. The liquor and frustration loosened his tongue. "What I'm trying to say is I'm getting nowhere with her. You're a guy; surely you understand what I'm saying."

Graham was on his feet in an instant, clenching and unclenching his fists. "I'm not the man to give you advice on this subject," he gritted out through clenched teeth as he towered above the table, "but I will say this." He pinned Robert with a threatening pewter stare. "As her 'brother' I'm counting on you to conduct yourself as a perfect gentleman." He called over his shoulder as he turned to leave. "And Robert, I'll be watching you."

❧

"Laura Wells, you look beautiful! That costume looks perfect, and I love your hair that way," Kathi circled her friend, studying her appearance. "I can't remember the last time you left your hair down. It looks terrific."

Laura smiled warmly at her vivacious friend. "Thank you," she lowered her eyes shyly. She wore a silky white Grecian gown that tied at one shoulder and draped in elegant folds to the floor. Her slender waist was encircled with a gold cord, and she wore a pair of delicate gold sandals on her feet.

"It's about time you stifled the accountant in you and let the softer side have full reign," Kathi said with an approving nod.

"This sounds silly," Laura spoke candidly, "but the somber colors and business clothes make me feel safe. They actually keep people at a respectful distance." She twisted the diamond bracelet at her wrist. "Being feminine makes me feel vulnerable, and frankly, a bit nervous."

Kathi stared a moment at her best friend, bright tears sparkling in her blue eyes. That whispered confidence was the first Laura had volunteered since the death of her mother nine long years ago. Kathi had dearly missed the close friendship they once shared. Was it possible that love had restored Laura to her old self? "You've really changed." Kathi's hushed voice was awed.

Laura nodded. "I've decided to take the risk of living, now that I don't face it alone." Suddenly embarrassed by the serious turn of the conversation, she sought to change the subject. "May I say you make an exceptional gypsy?"

Kathi turned gracefully on her toes, causing her brightly colored full skirt to swirl playfully around her calves. Her white peasant blouse and big, gold hoop earrings completed the look. "I think so, too. Now don't you think it's time we went down to the party? I can't wait to show off for the guys."

Laura hesitated for a split second. By successfully avoiding Graham, she hadn't suffered an erratic heartbeat all day. She knew seeing him would be painful. It would be so much easier to hide out in the room.

You'll have to face him sooner or later, she reminded herself. *After all, he's going to marry your best friend. And remember, you're not alone.* She squared her shoulders in firm resolve, "Let's go."

The costume party was held in a grand ballroom on the Viking Deck. Crewmen attired in crisp white uniforms greeted the guests. Laura and Kathi stepped inside the noisy room and stood on the top stair, momentarily transfixed.

A soldier in Confederate gray escorted an antebellum beauty across the floor. A six-foot alligator sauntered by them, carrying a plate of hors d'oeuvres in one hand and his scaly tail in the other.

Laura was amazed. She knew the costume party was billed as the biggest event during the week-long cruise, but she had not expected anything of this magnitude. It seemed to her that every passenger had turned out for the event, each dressed in a costume more elaborate than the one before.

There were monarchs Laura recognized from her history studies with their ladies in period gowns to match. She saw famous heroes and infamous villains, innocent maids and wily seductresses. The one person she did not see was the man whose very presence wreaked havoc with her heart.

"Well, well, what do we have here? Two lovely ladies to grace my humble table?"

The girls turned to face a slightly disheveled Robert dressed as a World War I flying ace. He executed a bow, and with debonair flair offered an arm to each girl, escorting them past long tables laden with food to a small, round table near the orchestra.

"Have you seen Graham?" Kathi practically shouted to be heard above the music and the reveling crowd.

Robert shook his head then turned his full attention to the woman beside him. "Laura, my beautiful goddess, your golden hair is painted with fiery glints of light."

Laura studied him for a moment, considering his uncharacteristic poetic bent. "Robert, have you been drinking?"

"A bit perhaps, but no alcohol could diminish your incredible beauty."

Kathi stifled a shocked giggle behind her hand. Laura shot her a warning look and leaned over to whisper to him, "I hope you won't be having any more. It appears to me you've had quite enough already."

"What?" Robert couldn't hear her above the din.

Laura leaned closer, resting her hand lightly on his shoulder, her mouth practically touching his ear. "I said, I think you have had enough to drink."

Robert took advantage of her position and wrapped an arm around her, pulling her close to his chest. He caught her off balance, and she fell against him with a startled gasp. As she struggled to sit up, Laura became aware of a fourth presence at the table.

"Good evening, ladies." Graham's deep voice carried smoothly. "Robert."

Laura pushed herself off of Robert in mortification. How humiliating to be caught in such a compromising position! She dropped her gaze to her hands, unwilling to look at Graham.

"Graham Kirkland, what you do for a Stetson and a pair of

jeans ought to be outlawed!" Kathi exclaimed. "My heart's all aflutter just looking at you."

Laura refused the temptation to look. She didn't want to see how handsome he looked. Just knowing he was nearby caused her breath to catch in her throat and her heart to race. She played absently with the catch on her bracelet. She couldn't hear his response to what she was sure was well deserved flattery, but she heard a velvety smooth chuckle and saw him squeeze Kathi's hand affectionately. Laura felt a familiar tug at her heartstrings. It was going to be a long night.

The four of them sat without speaking while a sea of noisy activity swirled around their table. For a time, Laura was content to study the costumes of the milling crowd. Finally, curiosity got the best of her, and she decided to take a quick peek at the forbidden cowboy seated across from her. He lounged sideways in his chair to watch the costumed revelers, and it offered her an opportunity to study him without being discovered.

Kathi was right. Graham looked magnificent. He wore a black felt cowboy hat pushed low on his dark brow and a shirt of weathered denim that fit his broad chest to perfection. Long muscular legs, sheathed in faded jeans, stretched out lazily before him. His bronze hands rested on the table, his long fingers drumming impatiently.

Laura wanted to look away—she'd had her quick peek—but her mutinous eyes refused, choosing instead to steal another glance at his handsome face. They traveled across his finely chiseled jaw dusted with a faint shadow of dark beard stubble and paused at his pursed mouth.

Even as she watched, his mouth relaxed into a broad smile, exposing even white teeth. Her heart skipped a beat. Slowly her eyes moved upward, and she found herself staring into his smiling eyes. She flushed deeply at being caught staring, but was unable to wrench her eyes away. He held her captive in his smoky gray gaze. She returned a shy smile.

Underneath the table, a hand gripped her knee and squeezed hard, startling Laura and causing her to jump in her chair. Her sudden movement drew both Graham's and Kathi's attention, and she flushed more deeply.

"It seems our pilot is flying tonight," Graham muttered with uncharacteristic sarcasm.

Laura glared at Robert who cackled happily beside her, seemingly oblivious to her displeasure. She was even more angry to hear Robert order another scotch. She'd seen him drink on occasion, but never to excess, and she was furious that he had chosen tonight to overdo.

An unpleasant thought struck her. She hadn't missed the scowls Graham continually directed toward him, nor had she missed his snide remark. In fact, there seemed to be an underlying hostility between the two men tonight. Suppose he and Graham were angry with one another over yesterday's trouble in St. Thomas? Perhaps Graham blamed Robert for her encounter with the robber. Her foolishness on the island may have caused a rift in their friendship.

No wonder Robert was into his cups, she thought. He had seemed to truly enjoy his association with Graham, and now he was hurting over the broken relationship. Her anger dissolved. She needed to help restore their friendship.

"Good evening, ladies and gentlemen," the captain stood at the microphone. "Welcome to the *SS Scandinavia* costume party. Tonight, it is my pleasure to present to you the finalists in our costume competition. You, the audience, will select the winners based on your applause."

For the next hour, the audience clapped for their favorite costumes in a variety of categories, and the winners were presented with gleaming trophies.

Laura had difficulty concentrating on the festivities. Robert and Graham continued to glare at one another, and she was more convinced than ever that the problem was her fault. She was anxious to get it resolved. Finally, with the presentation of the grand prize, the captain pronounced the competition ended and signaled the band to resume playing.

By now, Laura had formulated a plan. She leaned over to

Robert and whispered, "Can we talk? Privately?"

Robert nodded and tossed down the last of his drink with a few noisy gulps. She helped him to his feet, and together, they walked to a far corner of the room. His coordination was greatly impaired, and Laura caught herself before she laughed out loud at his spastic movements. The couples around them risked life and limb as he flailed his arms and legs with drunken abandon.

Laura moved close to Robert to be heard over the music. With surprising speed, Robert pulled her into his arms. He wrapped one arm around her slender waist and took her hand into his, pressing a wet kiss on her knuckles. "This is more like it," he spoke in a stage whisper, nuzzling her neck.

Laura suppressed a shudder of disgust, reminding herself that his pitiful condition was a direct result of her actions. She gently pushed him away. "Robert, we need to talk. Is there a problem between you and Graham?"

Robert withdrew from her slightly, trying to focus on her face. "Yes, there's a problem," his speech was slurred. "You."

He affirmed her fears. They were quarreling because of her. She felt horrible. "Oh, Robert, that's why you're drunk, isn't it?" she inquired, her soft, brown eyes filled with compassion. "Is there anything I can do?"

"Plenty." Robert pulled her close and pressed a moist kiss on her mouth.

Laura gasped and pushed him away again, this time holding him at arm's length. "Robert, please stop that. I want to talk."

Temporarily rebuffed, Robert released his tight grip on her. Laura assumed his response was an indication he was ready to discuss the problem. "Do you think that if I talked to Graham, I could straighten things out?"

Robert shook his head obstinately, "Not without me."

Laura conceded reluctantly. "Then let's go back to the table. I'm sure the three of us can straighten this out." The floor was crowded with costumed dancers, and Laura and Robert, under his drunken direction, bumped shoulders with countless other couples as they crossed the floor. Twice he stepped hard on her sandaled foot as he fought to maintain his balance. Laura glared at him, her patience rapidly waning. In response, Robert moved the hand that rested on her waist to caress her back and bent clumsily to kiss her neck.

"Robert, please. . ." Laura hissed between clenched teeth.

"Oh, Laura," he whispered hoarsely, "I want you. Don't you see it?"

Laura was repulsed by his roving hands and hot breath wreaking of scotch, and yet felt responsible for his inebriated condition. She wanted nothing more than to flee to the safety of her cabin and forget this night had ever happened. But first, she had to straighten things out between Graham and Robert. "Yes, Robert, I do see," she said with a forced laugh, "and so does everyone else, I'm sure."

"Tell me you want me," he pleaded. "I know you do. Just say it. You want me." By now, his voice was raised, and Laura was embarrassed to see several couples looking in their direction. This wasn't working. She needed a new strategy. Perhaps she should go back to the table and enlist Graham's help.

She tried to tell him she'd be right back, but he was quicker. He dragged her into an embrace and kissed her roughly, his hands moving behind her, caressing her boldly.

Suddenly, something inside Laura snapped, and she exploded. She wrenched herself away from him, her brown eyes flashing indignantly, and delivered a resounding slap across his leering face. Robert reeled backwards, crashing into a nearby couple, and fell to the floor, momentarily stunned. Laura gasped in horror as she watched him fall. By now, they were surrounded by a group of passengers who were laughing and jeering at Robert's prostrate figure. "Way to go, little lady!"

Laura felt sick. Painful memories of her fraternity date rushed before her. In a panic, she turned on her heel and fled through the crowd, running blindly across the dance floor, up the stairs, and out into the hall.

"Ma'am, can I help you?" The crewman at the door called after her retreating figure.

Laura shook her head, refusing to slow down to speak, in fear that Robert would be following close behind. She continued down the corridor at a full run, her gown wrapping ponderously around her ankles, not fully certain as to where she was headed.

When she reached the end of the hall she realized she had somehow missed the elevators and was now trapped at a dead end. She could hear pounding footfalls coming behind her. *Robert.* A door marked "Ship Personnel" caught her attention. Without hesitating, she yanked open the door and ducked into a dimly lit stairwell.

Her heart was racing, and she could hear her pulse throbbing in her ears. She dropped breathlessly onto the bottom stair. She could hear footsteps approaching the door. He sounded very close. "Laura? Laura baby, where are you?" Robert called drunkenly.

Laura sat stock still, her heart pounding wildly in her chest. She had no intention of calling out to him. She was so humiliated, she'd rather die. She listened as he continued to call for her. Gradually, his voice grew fainter as he moved farther from the stairwell, and Laura relaxed slightly.

She drew her knees up and hugged them tightly to her chest. Hot tears of humiliation coursed down her cheeks. "What a mess I've made of everything." She lay her head on her knees and wept bitterly.

"Laura?" The deep silky voice startled her, sending chills down her spine.

Laura wondered how long she'd been sitting there. She opened her swollen eyes a crack to see two scuffed boots standing at the foot of the stairs. She didn't need to look up to know who they belonged to.

"Laura, honey, are you hurt?"

Laura shook her head and wiped away her tears with the back of her hand. Graham reached down and gently lifted her to her feet. His gray eyes anxiously searched her face.

"You're late," she sniffled.

Graham looked bewildered. "Late?"

Laura nodded and turned a tear-streaked face to him. "You're supposed to rescue me before I get in trouble, not after." She offered him a weak smile.

Graham groaned softly and drew her to his chest, enveloping her in the protective circle of his strong arms. He stroked her hair tenderly. Laura leaned against him, the soft denim of his shirt caressing her cheek. The steady beat of his heart matched her own, and she sighed contentedly. This was the second time in two days that she'd found herself cradled in his arms, and it felt so right.

Her conscience reminded her Graham belonged to another, but she did not release him. Instead, she snuggled against him more closely, her arms wrapping around his waist. *Just a minute more,* she told herself, *I need to be held just a minute more.*

Graham broke the peaceful silence with a husky whisper, "Laura?"

Laura raised mahogany eyes to his, her dark lashes thick with tears. For a long moment, their eyes held. Graham's gaze dropped to her upturned lips. Slowly and gently he lowered his mouth to hers and kissed her with exquisite tenderness. Laura's arms wrapped around his neck as his lips continued to move on hers. She felt dizzy. Her mind was reeling with joy. She loved him so much.

Reality hit like a bolt of lightning. Kathi loved Graham, too, and Graham returned Kathi's love, not hers. Laura pulled away in abject horror, her face still flushed with the emotion of the kiss. "Oh, Graham, what have I done?"

He tried to pull her close, but she was already moving toward the door. "Wait, Laura, we need to talk."

Laura refused to look at him, her face burning with shame. "I'm, I'm sorry. Things are so crazy. . ."

"We need to talk." His deep voice was strained.

She shook her head sadly. "No, there's nothing to say. I've made a terrible mistake, and I'm sorry." She pulled open the door and stepped into the deserted corridor. She hesitated with frustrated uncertainty, and Graham moved to her side. "The elevator is down the hall to your right," he answered her unspoken question humorlessly.

Laura ran to the elevator without looking back, her heart heavy with guilt. This time she had gone too far. She'd betrayed her best friend. She had to find Kathi and confess what she'd done.

sixteen

Laura paced the floor of her small cabin, wringing her hands and casting worried glances at the travel clock. It was after one A.M. Where was Kathi? She vacillated between the elation of knowing that after tonight she could finally stop the lies, and the sheer terror of knowing that first she had to look her best friend in the eyes and confess her transgression.

A dreaded thought loomed in the back of her mind. Suppose Kathi didn't forgive her. Laura had to admit she couldn't blame her if she decided to end their friendship. After all, deception is not a desirable quality in a best friend. Laura paced faster.

1:53 A.M. Laura heard whispered voices outside the door. *Graham and Kathi.* She swallowed hard; her pulse was racing, and her stomach was tied in knots. The time had come for the confrontation. She paced back and forth, waiting for Kathi to come in for the evening, but the muffled whispering continued. Finally, when Laura could stand it no longer, she took a deep breath, and threw open the door.

Kathi gasped in surprise at the sudden intrusion and tried to disentangle herself from an amorous embrace. "Laura, I didn't know you were still up." She raised a shaky hand to smooth her dark curls.

Laura stood dumbfounded, her mouth hanging open, her eyes darting from Kathi to her companion, back to Kathi. She simply stared.

Kathi cleared her throat. "Uh, Laura, you remember Jack Martin, don't you? Jack, you remember my friend, Laura?"

Laura ignored his outstretched hand; the shock of seeing him rendered her immobile. After another minute of awkward silence, she finally found her voice. "You're not Graham," she accused. "Where is Graham?"

Jack coughed uncomfortably. "I believe I'll be going. Seems like you ladies have a lot to talk about."

"Thanks, Jack." Kathi smiled her appreciation. "See you tomorrow." He bent and placed a chaste kiss on her cheek, then disappeared down the hall.

Kathi took a bewildered Laura by the arm and guided her back into the cabin, closing the door behind them. "Sit down, Laura. There's so much I need to tell you."

"But, it wasn't Graham. You weren't with Graham," Laura repeated stupidly, while moving obediently to sit at the foot of her bed.

Kathi smiled with amused patience. "No, I wasn't with Graham. . ." she began slowly.

"But I thought. . ."

Kathi sat beside her on the bed, taking Laura's hands into her own. "I know you thought I was with him, and I'm sorry. I deliberately mislead you into thinking I was dating Graham."

Laura felt the room spin crazily. She shook her head as if to argue. "But you told me you loved him. Remember? You said he's the one."

Kathi nodded, her blue eyes locked onto Laura's confused brown ones. "That's true, I did love him, or at least I thought I did, and I wanted to make him love me." She smiled wistfully. "He wasn't interested, however. It seems his heart is already spoken for."

"But. . ."

"Let me try to explain. You see, after I realized there wasn't any future for Graham and me," she said, lowering her eyes. "Actually, after Graham told me there was no future for us, I knew I still had to keep him occupied, you know, out of the way so he wouldn't interfere with you and Robert. I know you, Laura. You feel responsible for Graham being here, and you'd feel obligated to entertain him, even at the cost of your relationship with Robert."

She met Laura's gaze and nodded solemnly. "You've changed, Laura, and I know that being in love with Robert is the reason." She squeezed Laura's hands tightly. "I just wanted to be sure nothing would get in the way of true love. I'm so sorry I lied to you, but I promise, I did it for you. You do forgive me, don't you?"

For a long moment, Laura said nothing; she just stared at her friend. Suddenly, she began to laugh, softly at first, blossoming into a hearty laugh that brought tears to her eyes. Kathi became alarmed. This wasn't like the Laura she knew.

"Laura," she said, "What is so funny?"

Laura struggled to catch her breath. "I'm not in love with Robert," she choked out between gales of laughter. "I was just trying to keep out of the way for you and Graham." She erupted into another fit of uncontrollable laughter.

"I don't understand." It was Kathi's turn to be thoroughly confused. "You have changed, you can't deny it. In fact, when I noticed the change, I even asked you if the changes were due to the new man in your life and you said they were."

Laura sobered. "There is a new man in my life, but it's certainly not Robert." She suppressed a shudder at the memory of his inept fondling that evening. For a long moment, she stared self-consciously at her hands, embarrassed to share something so personal. "It's God."

Kathi gasped. Laura was afraid to look at her. She twisted her bracelet nervously as she continued, "I've decided to become a Christian, and I asked Jesus to be my Savior." She glanced nervously at Kathi for her reaction, and found her smiling, her blue eyes twinkling merrily, as though she were about to laugh. Somewhat intimidated by her response, but determined to be honest, she persisted. "The change you see in me is God. He has given me something that I have lacked ever since my mother died. Peace."

Kathi began to giggle, and Laura flushed bright red. She hadn't expected Kathi to applaud her decision, but she hadn't expected to be laughed at, either. "I'm sorry you feel that way. I hoped you'd want to be a Christian, too."

"Oh, Laura," Kathi giggled as she reached over to embrace her. "I'm not laughing at you. I'm laughing at me."

Laura raised a questioning brow.

"You never asked me who Graham is stuck on," Kathi said with a mischievous grin. "Aren't you even a little curious?"

Laura's heart sank. She was very curious, but at the same time, she wasn't sure she wanted to know.

"Let me give you a clue. She's a tall, gorgeous blond from back home. Very intelligent. He is forever telling me about her incredible eyes." She looked at Laura with a wry smile. "I'm pretty sick of hearing about her eyes, if you want to know the truth. It's been quite a strain on my fragile ego."

Laura felt sick, too. She wanted to cry. "I'm not sure I want to hear any more. . ."

"She's been tied up with someone else until very recently," Kathi continued, heartlessly ignoring Laura's plea. "In fact, she doesn't even know how Graham feels about her."

Laura's heart went out to Graham. He was suffering the very same heartache she was. "Why doesn't he tell her how he feels?"

"Oh, he's a man of integrity. He wouldn't consider interfering." Kathi leaned toward Laura and whispered confidentially, "The real shame of it is her best friend knows, has known for a long time how he feels about her, but she didn't tell. She was of the opinion that the two just wouldn't suit. Him being a holy roller and all that."

"Oh," Laura said in a very small voice. Up until a few days ago, she held the very same opinion.

"I need to ask you a question. How do you feel about our chaperone?" Kathi asked with a sly smile.

Laura flushed crimson, and dropped her eyes guiltily.

Kathi laughed. "That answers my question quite nicely. Now, if you'll be kind enough to turn those 'incredible' eyes toward me, there's something I think you ought to know."

Laura complied without understanding, shyly raising her gaze.

"It's you, Laura. Graham is in love with you!"

Laura felt her heart stop, then leap wildly within her chest. She grasped Kathi's hands with a grip that threatened to cut off the blood supply. "What do you mean he's in love with me? I mean, are you sure?"

Kathi giggled. "Yes, I am sure. Haven't you been listening? For days now, all he can talk about is you."

"But, but, I didn't know," Laura stammered.

Kathi became serious, her blue eyes forlorn. "I'm so sorry. It's all my fault. I was trying to help, and I'm afraid I've made a mess of things. I thought you were madly in love with Robert; in fact, I told Graham that several times. I knew Graham cared for you, but I figured there was no point in muddying the water by telling you. After all, you were happily in love—at least I thought you were—and I knew you'd never be interested in Graham, him being the religious kind." Kathi took a deep breath. "I guess I've meddled a bit too much. Will you ever forgive me?"

Laura threw her arms around Kathi and hugged her. "Forgive you? I adore you! You've made me the happiest person in the world." Suddenly, Laura stopped. "Oh no, I need to talk to Graham and straighten things out." She started to rise from the bed. "I wonder if he's in his cabin?" she mused aloud.

Kathi grabbed her arm and pulled her back to the bed. "Laura, it's 2:30 in the morning. Don't you think this could wait till a more reasonable hour?"

Laura nodded grudgingly. Kathi was probably right, but she didn't want to wait. She wanted to see him right now. Her fingers absently traced her lips as she remembered the tender kiss he'd given her. He loved her, and she wanted to tell him she loved him. She felt so happy, she thought she might burst. Graham loved her. Her overworked heart was doing cartwheels.

"Now," Kathi interrupted her reverie, "tell me all about your new man."

"Well, you already know he's gorgeous, kind, and intelligent..."

"Not Graham, you goof. I meant God!" Kathi laughed.

Laura flushed with embarrassment. Kathi laughed harder at her bemused, lovesick friend, and Laura joined in good-naturedly. "I'm glad you asked about Him," she said a bit breathlessly. "I want you to know Him, too."

Thirty minutes later, after Laura had shared simply from her heart the things she knew to be true about her heavenly Father, the girls knelt together beside the bed, and Kathi gave her heart to God.

"Do you think you can stand having me around for eternity?" Kathi teased.

Laura replied with a laugh, "I'm certain heaven will never be the same."

By the time the girls finally climbed into their beds, Laura was exhausted. Happy, but exhausted.

"You know, Kathi," Laura commented across the darkened room, "You never told me how you met up with Jack Martin. I haven't seen him anywhere on the ship."

Kathi sat up to answer. "I was with Graham when we ran into him. Jack is the personal trainer at the gym. He works from noon till midnight, so you wouldn't see him at any functions."

Laura smiled to herself. So that's why Kathi was getting back so late. Jack didn't get off work until midnight. "What in the world were you and Graham doing at the gym, anyway?"

"Poor Graham was having trouble with stiffness," Kathi said, and then paused momentarily in recollection. "Overexertion is what Jack called it, I think. Anyway, Graham wanted to get in the whirlpool, and it's at the gym. I was just tagging along with him when we saw Jack." She sighed dreamily. "So while Graham soaked, Jack and I visited. Pretty romantic, huh?"

Laura smiled to herself. *Only Kathi could find romance in a gym.* "I'd like to get to know Jack better, although I'm afraid I didn't give him a very good impression this evening." Laura grimaced. "He must think I'm a dolt."

Kathi giggled. "You did look pretty surprised at the door, but I'm sure he understood. I've explained to him all about us." Laura groaned in dismay, but Kathi continued gaily, "He's off on Saturday. Maybe the four of us could double date."

Laura smiled in the dark. "I'd like that."

seventeen

Graham dragged himself out onto the jogging track, his entire body rebelling. Not because of the stiffness that had recently plagued him, the whirlpool had cured him quite nicely. It wasn't anything physical at all. He just felt miserable.

Last night when he had held Laura in his arms and kissed her, and she had seemed to return his affection, he'd harbored the hope that Kathi was mistaken about Laura and Robert, that perhaps Laura cared for him. That hope had been dashed when she had pulled away, her beautiful face contorted with disgust. He could still hear her saying, "I'm sorry. There's nothing to talk about. It was a mistake." Thinking about it this morning caused his heart to lurch sickeningly within his chest. It might be a mistake, but he couldn't help it. He loved her.

He started to run around the deserted track, deriving a perverse pleasure from torturing his body. He knew Laura wouldn't be there. The last two mornings, he had been there, waiting for her, but she hadn't come. He realized in retrospect, she was probably avoiding him.

Graham ran faster, pushing himself at a punishing speed. Rounding the first curve, he caught sight of another runner, the first he'd seen this morning. His heart leaped in his chest. *Laura.* It had to be her; he'd recognize her anywhere.

For a moment he slowed his pace, deliberating whether to speak to her or go back to his cabin. *I'll keep my distance,* he promised himself, *I just want to see her. That will be enough.* With a burst of speed he did not know himself capable of, Graham thundered to her side.

Laura heard a runner advancing from behind, and she moved to allow him to pass. Her heart skipped a beat when she saw who the runner was. She prayed she'd find him on the track. "Someone chasing you?" she teased, noting his speed.

Graham was obviously not in the mood for small talk. "Laura, I'm sorry about last night." His tone was grave, and his eyes were trained straight ahead.

"You are?" She stole a quick glance at him, and seeing his expression, she, too, averted her eyes to the front.

Graham didn't miss the disappointment in her voice. "Yes," he glanced over at her, "shouldn't I be? I mean, after all, you and Robert are. . ." He couldn't make himself finish.

"Well, yes, I guess you should be sorry if Robert and I are. . ." Laura mimicked his inflection. "But we're not."

"Oh, I see."

The two of them continued running, their pace never varying during the exchange. Suddenly, Graham stopped dead in his tracks. "Say that again?"

Laura smiled. "I said, Robert and I are not!"

Graham's dark brow furrowed. "But last night, after I kissed you, you said you were sorry, it was all a mistake."

"I thought you and Kathi were. . ."

"But we're not."

"I know. Kathi and I had a long talk last night."

Graham was silent for a moment, analyzing the information he had just received. "You and Robert are not?"

Laura nodded, her brown eyes twinkling merrily at their cryptic conversation. "Right."

Graham's arms were around her in a flash, pulling her into a bone-crushing embrace. He raised his eyes toward heaven. *Thank You,* he mouthed in silent gratitude. He loosened his grip slightly, and Laura looked into his face with such tenderness mirrored in her dark eyes that Graham felt his knees weaken. He lowered his mouth to hers, savoring the touch of her soft, full lips. Laura sighed contentedly.

"Hey, kids! Can't you do that neckin' somewhere else?" a passing runner scolded them good-naturedly.

Laura stiffened and drew back instantly, her face flushing a bright crimson.

Graham chuckled deeply. "As much as I'd like to continue this," he said with a heart-stopping grin, "I think we should talk. How about over breakfast?"

The knock-out combination of Graham's breath-taking kiss and killer smile left Laura light-headed and weak-kneed. She gave him a feeble nod and trailed obediently behind him on wobbly legs.

The sun had already begun its ascent, reflecting off the endless sea as a thousand glittering gems. A welcome breeze whipped the taut canvas of the bright, orange umbrella that shaded Graham and Laura from the sun's scorching rays.

The two sat in awkward silence, the plates of mouthwatering food before them remaining untouched. Graham mentally chided himself. Sitting before the woman he loved, he found himself hopelessly tongue-tied. He hadn't felt this inadequate since he had asked Mary Jane Flimverten to the senior prom. He chuckled lightly at the disastrous memory.

Laura looked up at the warm sound of his laugh. Their eyes met, and she smiled shyly. Graham's bronze hand moved over to rest on hers.

"Laura," Graham began in a gravelly voice he didn't recognize as his own. He grinned in embarrassment, cleared his throat, and tried again. "It's funny, I've rehearsed over and over in my mind the things I wanted to say to you, and I've prayed for the opportunity to say them, and now that I have it, I find myself nervous."

Laura nodded with unspoken empathy, her eyes locked on his. He rallied to the encouragement he found there, "I. . ."

"I thought I'd find you love birds out here!" Kathi called brightly as she sprang toward the table. "And I see that I am right on time, you haven't started to eat yet. Mind if I join you?" She placed her well-filled plate on the table. "I'm not interrupting anything, am I?"

Kathi missed the helpless shrug of Graham's broad shoulders. Reminding himself that he was a gentleman, he rose to hold Kathi's chair for her. "We'd love for you to join us," came his mechanical, if unenthusiastic, reply.

Laura couldn't decide if she should laugh or cry. Opting to be cheerful, she said, "You're up awfully early."

"I figured the three of us could spend the day together, and I knew if I didn't catch up with you at breakfast that I may not see you again until four." She looked over at Laura's plate. "Better eat up before the food gets cold."

Following an amiable breakfast spent almost entirely in a discussion of what to do for the rest of the day, the party split up. Laura and Kathi headed for their room to change into their swimsuits, and Graham departed for his. Twenty minutes later, they met at their rendezvous point on the Sun Deck for a leisurely day by the pool.

The Sun Deck was as yet uncrowded, and Laura guided them to her customary spot near the railing where they commandeered three white lounge chairs.

After dropping his belongings on his chair, Graham turned to study the pool. "The water looks great. How about a swim?"

Laura laid her beach bag on the chair beside his. "I'd love to."

"Not for me, thanks," Kathi said with a shake of her dark curls. "I hate to get chlorine in my hair. You two go on, and I'll chaperone from here." She plopped into her chair and promptly buried her nose in the latest fashion magazine.

Graham was already headed for the water when he called over his shoulder, "Race you to the pool!"

Laura gave him a good race and would perhaps have beaten him had she not been doubled over with laughter at the sight of him hurdling the scattered chairs in his path. Graham plunged headfirst into the water, with Laura trailing close behind. The water was cool and refreshing, and they spent a pleasant hour frolicking and splashing like carefree porpoises.

By the time they emerged from the pool, ready to dry off, they had accumulated a sizable audience of sunbathers who watched their antics with amusement.

If only we could be alone, Laura despaired. There was so much she wanted to say to Graham and even more that she wanted to hear. However, it was obvious that their conversation would have to wait until a more private time.

"You two look like drowned rats!" Kathi pronounced affectionately as they returned to their chairs.

I couldn't disagree more, Laura thought as she fondly studied the waterlogged man at her side. Even sopping wet, he was everything she'd ever dreamed of: the epitome of tall, drenched, and handsome.

* * *

Graham arrived promptly at eight to escort the girls to dinner. As per her usual evening ritual, Laura's stomach was queasy and her palms clammy. Even the welcome sight of Graham at the door didn't calm her fears. The source of her distress was the same as before. Robert. Dinner meant she would have to face Robert, and after last night she wasn't at all certain she ever wanted to see him again.

Laura clung to Graham's arm, steeling herself for the upcoming confrontation as they entered the dining room. To her immense relief, Robert was conspicuously absent from the table. "He's not here," she whispered her thoughts aloud.

"Probably hung over. He really tied one on last night. You're not disappointed, are you?" Graham's gray eyes studied her face.

"I'm delighted," she said with a happy grin as she took her place at the table across from Graham. "I'm not certain what I'd say to him."

Graham's gaze grew steely. "I have a few ideas."

"Graham Kirkland, you sound like you're jealous," Kathi teased. Laura said nothing, but inwardly her heart was soaring. Graham was jealous!

After polishing off a luscious dinner of Caesar salad, lobster thermidor, and a spicy pasta vegetable dish, topped off with an incredibly rich chocolate confection for dessert, the three of them were sated. The conversation which had flowed furiously over dinner slowed to a sporadic drizzle over coffee, each of them too full to speak.

Breaking a long silence, Kathi placed her empty coffee cup back in the saucer. "I noticed a very romantic moon this evening, on our way to dinner. I have my heart set on seeing the movie they're showing in the theater tonight, and then I'm going to meet Jack at the gym, so I won't be able to accompany you two on deck." She flashed a wicked smile. "Think you can handle things without me?" Without waiting for a reply, she excused herself from the table with another grin and disappeared through the double doors.

"Alone at last!" Graham declared with dramatic flourish. "Miss Wells, may I have the pleasure of your company topside?" His deep voice was silky smooth, his gray eyes sparkling mischievously. "I hear that there is a most compelling moon."

Delighted shivers of anticipation crept down her spine. "I'd be delighted, Mr. Kirkland."

She gave a contented little purr as she slipped her slender arm through his. She loved the feel of his sleeve against her arm, his clean masculine scent in her nostrils. *When you get right down to it,* she thought happily, *I love everything about him.* And, for the first time today, she had him all to herself. Maybe now they could finish what they'd started earlier. She couldn't decide what sounded better, the talking or the kissing!

They stepped out onto the International Deck, the same deck they had visited during their grand tour the first night of the cruise. It was lovely, a magical fairyland as before. The tables were topped with flickering candles, the torches burned brightly at their posts, and the thousands of tiny lights strung from the railing twinkled cheerfully in the twilight. Even the calypso band was performing as it had been that first night.

But tonight it was all different. In Laura's eyes, each light burned more brightly, each song was more beautiful, the magic of the deck was more pronounced. She was a part of the light-heartedness tonight. She was a Christian with the promise of God's peace, and she was in love.

Graham guided her to the railing and they stood side by side, studying the inky depths in silence. An insistent breeze ruffled her blond hair that she wore loosely about her shoulders and toyed with the hem of her full skirt, twisting it about her slender calves.

Graham brushed a strand of hair from her eyes, rubbing the silky tresses between his fingers. "Have I ever told you how lovely you are?"

Laura dropped her gaze, embarrassed by the praise.

"It's true. You are the loveliest woman I have ever met. And it's not just your physical beauty. There is a beauty radiating from within you." His voice dropped to a husky whisper. "I guess that's why I love you."

Laura's heart leaped within her chest. She turned velvet eyes to Graham. "I love you, too," she said, her voice a breathless whisper.

Graham's strong arms wrapped around her, drawing her into a tender embrace. He lowered his mouth, pressing his lips to hers. Laura's pulse was racing, and fireworks rivaling anything she'd ever witnessed were exploding in her brain. She felt her legs grow weak, as if her knees had become liquid, and for a fleeting moment, she thought she might melt.

"It's strange," he murmured against her lips, "I know we've only spent a few short days together, and yet I feel like I've known you all my life." There was a smile in his voice as he continued, "I was afraid to tell you I love you. I didn't want you to think it was a purely physical attraction."

He smiled warmly at her, his white teeth shining in stark contrast to his bronzed skin. He gave a low chuckle as he placed a finger under her chin and gently tipped it up, forcing her to meet his smokey gaze. "I'd be a liar if I didn't admit, however, that I do find you incredibly attractive."

Laura was glad for the cover of darkness that shrouded the blush she felt creeping across her cheeks. She was well aware of the electricity that charged the air between them, but she hadn't known he felt it too. Just hearing him say he was attracted to her made her light-headed. She had never been in love, and she found the whole thing a bit alarming.

Graham seemed to sense her discomfort. "I hope I haven't frightened you." His eyes sparkled merrily. "I promise I won't gobble you up."

Laura laughed softly, his teasing seeming to dispel her fears. And time together with the man she loved was too precious to waste on fear.

eighteen

Saturday, the final full day of the cruise, seemed to fly by, whisking Laura and the others along at a whirlwind pace. The *SS Scandinavia* was anchored in a quiet cove off the cruise line's own private island just southeast of Miami where the passengers could spend the day enjoying the tropical paradise.

Laura sat studying her reflection in the dressing table mirror while she applied a hint of pink lipstick to her lips. Her gaze moved dreamily beyond her image as she stared off into space. She sighed deeply.

For the most part, it had been a wonderful day. She and Graham, along with Kathi and Jack, had gone to the island early trying to make the most of their rapidly fleeting time together. They'd had a very full morning beginning with snorkeling out in the crystal clear water some thirty feet from shore.

Laura smiled at the memory. Jacques Cousteau she was not. She was pathetically awkward in her cumbersome flippers that sought repeatedly to topple her, and no matter how much moisture she deposited in her mask, she could not keep it clear.

Then, there was the matter of the snorkel. The process of breathing through a small tube that protruded only a few inches above the surface of the water did not come naturally to her. She grimaced at the memory of how much sea water she'd ingested in the one-hour time period. She felt reasonably sure the water level surrounding the island had receded several inches.

In spite of the technical difficulties she'd encountered, she'd loved it. The fish were interesting, but the best part was paddling along side-by-side with Graham. He never left her side as they studied the cove, choosing instead to hold her hand, offering her the protection of his nearness. Holding his hand, she felt invincible.

After snorkeling, the foursome had joined a rousing game of volleyball. The delicious aroma of grilling hamburgers brought a quick end to the game while the players adjourned for a picnic lunch under the swaying palms.

Jack distinguished himself as a world-class appetite, consuming four hamburgers and his weight in potato salad before his monstrous hunger abated. At the time, it was the subject of much good-natured joking, but Laura realized now that one could not sustain the bulk Jack did by eating like a bird.

Almost before she'd known it, the four of them were back in the ferry, skimming across the sapphire sea back to the ship to freshen up for dinner. They had the option of eating in the formal dining room on board or taking part in a luau on the island, and they all agreed the luau sounded like fun.

Laura returned her gaze to her reflection. Absently, she picked up her hairbrush and began to brush her golden hair to a silky sheen. Her mind continued to wander.

Tonight was their final night on the cruise. Within the coming week, she would begin her new job with Cunningham and Associates. Graham would be back at the helm of his family business. Job demands would replace early morning runs and late night walks. Laura frowned into the mirror. Graham wouldn't be there to hold her hand as she traveled new uncharted waters.

A sadness settled over her. The same sadness that had tormented her all day, hurling melancholy thoughts at her when she was still. Things were going to change, she knew that. They couldn't take the jeweled sea or tropical breezes home with them. But what if Graham's feelings changed? What if their new-found love paled in the light of business and real world pressures? She sighed again.

"What's the matter?" Kathi asked, rubbing a towel over her wet hair as she stepped from the bathroom.

Laura shrugged, "Nothing, I guess." She paused, and then amended, "Well, maybe a case of the vacation-end blues."

Kathi walked over and rested her hands gently on Laura's shoulders. "I feel the same way. In fact, I have all day. But I had this weird thought in the shower. We're Christians now, right?"

Laura nodded.

"What do Christians do when they're sad or worried?"

Laura sat thinking for a moment. Suddenly, her eyes met Kathi's in the mirror. "They pray! I'm embarrassed I didn't think of it before." With that, she moved to the nightstand and began flipping through Graham's Bible. "I saw a passage in here the other night," she paused to skim the page, "Here it is! Philippians 4:6,7."

Kathi sat on the bed beside her to listen.

"Do not be anxious about anything, but in everything, by prayer and petition, with thanksgiving, present your requests to God. And the peace of God, which transcends all understanding, will guard your hearts and your minds in Christ Jesus."

Laura plopped on the bed. A light of understanding gleamed in her dark eyes. "That's it! That's the reason I only have sporadic peace. I thought once I became a Christian that the peace just stayed. But it didn't." She looked steadily at Kathi. "Do you know why?"

Kathi shook her head in bewilderment.

"Because I chose to worry and not to pray. It says here to pray and then you get the peace." She flopped back on the bed. "No wonder I felt like I was on an emotional roller coaster. I'd forgotten my heavenly Father." She sat up with a surge of energy and hugged Kathi tightly. "You're wonderful!"

Kathi beamed, still not exactly certain what she'd done to earn such high praise. "I've been telling you that all along."

Laura giggled in exasperation and dropped to her knees, motioning Kathi to kneel beside her.

"You pray," Kathi whispered. "I'm not exactly sure what to say."

Laura bowed her head. "Heavenly Father, forgive me for forgetting you. And thank You for Kathi's reminder. Thank You too that You are always here with us, ready to listen and give us Your peace. You know what Kathi and I are feeling, probably better than we do." Laura paused. "I don't even know the specifics to pray. I don't know what Your will is for us. But I trust You know best."

She paused again, searching for the right words to express her heart's desire. "I just ask that. . .that we live happily ever after."

"Amen!" Kathi declared in a loud voice.

Laura felt immeasurably better. The simple prayer lightened her heart and lifted her spirits. Kathi's, too. By the time Jack and Graham arrived at the door, the girls were positively giddy.

Graham stood at the door of the cabin studying the two glowing faces before him. "Why do I get the impression you enjoyed our absence?" he questioned, feigning injury.

Laura mimicked the outrageous flirtation she'd witnessed so often in her best friend. She opened her dark eyes wide, fluttering her lashes coyly. "Nonsense, it was the anticipation of seeing you handsome men that has us all a-twitter."

Graham threw back his head and roared laughter. "'All a'twitter' my eye." Before he could stop himself, he pulled her into an embrace and dropped a resounding kiss on her upturned mouth. "And let that be a lesson to you, young lady," he teased. "If I ever find you looking so beautiful again, I'll do the very same thing."

This time it was Laura's turn to laugh as her heart nearly burst with joy.

The four of them bantered amiably, joking and laughing as they traveled down through the ship and out onto the waiting ferry. Strings of tiny, white lights decorated the ferry in honor of the evening's luau. In the distance, the island glowed with the light of hundreds of flickering torches, and the joyful sound of calypso music met their ears as it carried across the rolling water.

Laura's pulse raced along with the ferry as they skimmed toward shore. She couldn't remember ever being so happy. Everything was so exciting. It wasn't that she had forgotten it was her last night of the cruise. It was that she had remembered to seek God's peace. And she'd found it.

As the ferry moored at the dock, Graham stepped out first and bent to assist Laura as she disembarked. His strong hand grasped hers, steadying her as she stepped onto the dock.

He studied her closely, as if noticing her apparel for the very first time. "Is this the dress you bought in St. Thomas?" He smiled appreciatively. "It's a knockout!"

Laura met his eyes and smiled a shy smile. "I'm glad you like it." She too had been very pleased when she had seen her reflection in the mirror earlier. She hadn't paid very close attention in the shop, she had been in such a hurry to leave, but the rosy color was the perfect complement to her own coloring, highlighting her natural blush. The fitted bodice and long gracefully flaring skirt that brushed her calves fit like a glove.

"Like it?" He leaned his handsome head toward her and whispered mischievously, "I may have trouble keeping my promise not to gobble you up."

Laura did not have the opportunity to respond, for at that moment, a second ferry from the ship pulled up to the dock, and the passengers began to unload. A familiar face caught Laura's attention. "Robert!" she gasped, quickly turning her back to him in hopes that he would not notice her. "I forgot all about him."

Graham smiled broadly as he tucked her slender arm possessively through his. "Oh, him," his voice was casual. "I ran into him this afternoon, and we had the opportunity to chat." He gave a low chuckle. "We came to an understanding, and I'm certain he won't give you any problems."

Laura turned a grateful gaze to him. "My hero," she giggled, shaking her head in amazement. "You'll never know how many times you've rescued me from him this week."

You'd be surprised, Graham thought, but he chose to say nothing, answering instead with a grin.

"I'm starved!" Jack exclaimed, "Let's eat."

They headed down the dock with the other passengers toward the festivities. Heavenly smells of roasting meat assaulted them, and Laura felt her own stomach rumble with hunger. The four of them followed the crowd to the dining room, which was nothing more than a level area of beach, the perimeter of which was marked by squadrons of glowing torches standing in formation. To Laura's mind, it was a fairy land.

A crewmen in full uniform guided them to long tables decorated with lush flowers and heavily laden with every kind of food imaginable. Jack sighed a contented sigh, and rubbed his hands together in delighted anticipation, causing Graham to suggest with a laugh, "Jack, perhaps the ladies and I should go first, and then you can finish up what's left."

After filling their plates to capacity in the buffet line, they located a table for four. Laura smiled. Even on a tropical island, with sand for a floor, the cruise line provided elegant dining with linen-covered tables and candlelight.

Conversation over dinner was deliberately lighthearted. It was almost as if no one wanted to be serious, to venture into the future and spoil the mood. Each was determined to enjoy the moment while he could.

Laura thought that Graham was more quiet than usual, as though he were preoccupied. Several times she glanced toward him and found him staring off into space, as though he were a million miles away. The moment he became aware of her worried look, he would smile. That same heart-stopping smile that stole her breath and effectively muddled her thoughts so completely that she couldn't remember what it was that concerned her.

Four helpings later, Jack leaned back in his chair, patted his stomach, and pronounced dinner concluded.

"Laura and I are going for a walk, to digest our dinner." Graham turned to Laura, "If it's all right with you?"

She melted under his gray gaze. "Um hum," she murmured dreamily, rejoicing in the opportunity to be alone with him.

He took her hand and together they passed through the crowded dining room and out across the beach to the shore. They slipped off their shoes and piled them at a safe distance from the water. Graham rolled up the legs of his khakis.

They walked hand-in-hand along the beach, traveling far enough from the noise of the luau that the only sound to be heard was that of the water lapping rhythmically on the sand. The two of them were silent, savoring the peaceful serenity of the evening. While outwardly calm, inwardly Laura's heart soared, rejoicing over the nearness of Graham, the wonderful feeling of his hand enveloping her own. This was heavenly.

"Do you consider me a rational man?" Graham's deep voice pummeled the silence.

The question startled Laura. "Rational? Yes, I think you are rational."

Graham stopped and took both her hands in his, his gray eyes locking onto hers. "Good. Because there's something I'd like to ask you, and I wanted to be certain that you knew me to be of sound mind."

Laura's pulse was racing. The smoky look he leveled on her caused her knees to wobble, and his proximity caused her head to spin. She could scarcely think. "Sound mind?" she giggled absently as she studied his handsome face, concentrating more on how nice it would be to be kissed by those lips than on what the lips were saying. "Are you asking me to witness your last will and testament?"

"No. I am asking you to marry me."

Laura's pulse was throbbing so loudly in her ears, she wasn't certain she'd heard him correctly. "I beg your pardon?" she whispered, seeking confirmation.

Graham mistook her question as one of incredulity. "I was afraid you'd feel that way, us knowing each other such a short time. But I've prayed about it—really sought God's wisdom, and I am absolutely certain I'll love you for a lifetime. Just as certain as I am that I cannot possibly function until I know that you will be mine, forever." He paused, his eyes studying her intently. "I love you, Laura."

Laura opened her mouth to respond, but Graham interrupted, not ready to hear her rejection. "I'll be reasonable. Since we've had such a short courtship, we can have a long engagement, if you want. I just have to know that one day you'll be the first thing I see in the morning, and the very last thing I see at night."

"Graham!" Laura blurted out, before he could interrupt again. "I'm not refusing you. I just asked you to repeat the question."

Graham's grip on her hands relaxed somewhat. Intense gray eyes held hers. "Will you marry me?"

Laura nodded briskly. "Yes. . ."

He swept her into his strong arms and whirled her around until she was breathless. Finally, he lowered her feet to the ground and gently drew her to him, their lips meeting in a long, tender kiss.

"Whew," Graham whispered huskily as their lips parted, "let's don't make it too long an engagement."

Laura's head was reeling. Graham loved her and wanted to marry her. This was more wonderful than anything she could have asked for. When God answered prayer, He didn't mess around.

Long into the night they sat there in the warm sand, under the twinkling stars, talking and laughing, sharing their innermost thoughts and dreams.

"It's funny," Laura's voice was a dreamy whisper, "I've been dreading the thought of being apart from you when we get back home. It's such a little thing, but I didn't want to give up seeing you first thing in the morning for our run." She lay her head against his broad shoulder. "Won't it be great? Now we can be running partners for life."

Graham sat up slightly, and groaned. "Laura, I have a confession to make."

Laura turned her gaze to his, and quirked a finely arched brow. "Yes?"

He stared guiltily at the ground. "I'm not a runner. In fact, I hate to run." He amended that slightly, "Or rather, I did hate to run until this week. . ."

"You hate to run? I don't believe it. If you hate to run then why did you even come out to the track?"

"Your father had told me that if I wanted to get an opportunity to talk with you, I'd better catch you during your morning run."

"Graham Kirkland! Do you mean to tell me that you and my father cooked the whole thing up?" She considered his guilty expression for a moment. "Now I'm beginning to understand. That morning when I thought you were limping, you were limping. And that's why you were in the whirlpool."

Graham chuckled at the memory. "I wasn't just limping, I was dying. If it hadn't been for the whirlpool, I'm afraid the cruise line would have had a burial at sea this week—for me." His smile faded as he considered her thoughtful expression. "You're not angry with me are you?"

Laura threw her arms around his shoulders and hugged him tightly. "Angry? No, I'm flattered. You went through an awful lot of pain for me, just to talk to me. My father doesn't realize what a devoted friend he has."

"We'd better be getting back," Graham said with a reluctant glance over his shoulder. "It's late and I don't want us to miss the last boat to the ship."

They strolled back along the water, arms entwined, enjoying the cool sensation as the waves washed over their feet. Within minutes, they sighted the luau, where only a few stout-hearted revelers remained.

Graham gathered their shoes from the pile where they had left them earlier and the two of them headed up the nearly deserted dock to the waiting ferry.

"Oh ho! It's the lovebirds!" Laura recognized the speaker as the same crewman that had ferried them twice before. "Aren't you two out a little late without a chaperone?" he teased.

"He is my chaperone," Laura said with a laugh. "Anyway, it's okay, we're going to be married."

The joking crewman beamed. "It's the sea air. Works every time." He shook Graham's hand, offering him his hearty congratulations.

They lingered at the door of Laura's cabin, neither willing to call an end to a perfect day.

"Oh!" Graham began fumbling in his pocket. "I almost forgot." He withdrew a small box and handed it to Laura. "I bought this earlier, in hope that you would agree to be my wife."

Laura stood motionless, holding the black velvet box in the palm of her hand.

"Aren't you going to open it?"

With trembling fingers, Laura slowly lifted the hinged lid exposing a ring set with a large, oval, blue sapphire surrounded by a wreath of sparkling diamonds.

"It's beautiful!" Laura gasped as bright moisture filled her eyes.

Graham detected the tears. "I hope you like it. I know it's not your ordinary engagement ring. I must have looked at a hundred of them in the jewelry store downstairs, but I couldn't find one that was just right." He smiled a broad smile, his white teeth gleaming. Gently, he tipped her face to his and planted a light kiss on her nose. "I guess it's because you are not an ordinary woman."

Laura smiled through the welling tears.

"Anyway, I like the sapphire. It reminds me of the ocean. A place that will hold a special meaning for me always." He slipped the ring out of its box and slid it onto her finger.

"It fits," she whispered as a tear rolled down her cheek.

"What's the matter, honey? Don't you like the ring? Am I pushing things too fast?"

"Nothing's the matter," she sniffled. "In fact, everything is so wonderful, I guess that's why I'm crying." She turned teary eyes to meet his. "A week ago my life was in total chaos. I wasn't even certain I wanted to live. Yet, in a few short days, I'm happier than I have ever been. You've introduced me to the love of my heavenly Father, and He, in turn, has provided me with the perfect man to love. God is so good."

Graham drew her into his arms and held her tightly as he looked heavenward and nodded his agreement. *God is so good.*

nineteen

Laura and Graham were on the jogging track at 6 A.M. sharp Sunday morning. He seemed to miss the impish grin that played at the corner of her lips. In retaliation for his deception about being a runner, Laura decided to run extra hard, setting a grueling pace for him to match. After keeping up nicely for two full laps, meeting her stride for stride, Graham suddenly groaned sharply as his legs collapsed beneath him.

Laura saw him fall and her heart hammered fearfully within her chest. "Oh, Graham!" she cried out in panic as she fell to her knees, cradling his head in her lap. His eyes were closed, his dark lashes fanning across his cheeks and his handsome mouth contorted with pain.

"I'm so sorry," she whispered tenderly as she stroked a dark curl from his forehead. "I shouldn't have pushed you so hard. I was only teasing, trying to get back at you for saying you were a runner." Frantically, she searched the deck for someone to help her get him to a doctor.

Without warning two strong arms wrapped around her neck, pulling her down into an embrace and just before her lips met his, she caught a glimpse of sparkling, gray eyes and a dazzling smile.

"You two kids at it again?" the same runner who had witnessed their kiss yesterday asked with a grin as he trotted by. "Isn't there some place you could go that would be more comfortable?"

Laura drew back with an embarrassed start, flushing to the soles of her feet. Graham burst out laughing, a deep hearty laugh that proved contagious, sweeping Laura into the hilarity.

"You're a beast," she scolded, when she was able to draw a breath. "You frightened me out of my wits!"

"And you, madam," Graham returned, with a merry blue glint

164

in his gray eyes, "are equally beastly for torturing me. Another lap like that, and I would have required a stretcher to carry me from the ship."

Laura raised her hands in playful surrender. "I call a truce."

"Agreed." Graham rose to his feet and pulled Laura to a standing position. "And we can draw up the terms over breakfast."

After enjoying a leisurely breakfast out on the International Deck, they attended church together in a tiny chapel deep within the ship. Kneeling beside Graham in silent prayer, Laura was once again filled with a deep sense of awe and gratitude to her heavenly Father.

She was not the same person that had boarded the ship a week ago. That woman, the lonely, fearful Laura, was gone. A new Laura, a woman of peace and hope, had taken her place.

Just as the glossy travel brochures had promised, the cruise had proved to be life changing. She didn't need a wall around her for protection any more. She smiled with the confidence that with God before her and Graham beside her, she was invincible.

To close the brief service, the chaplain read a passage from 2 Corinthians 5:17. Laura knew the moment she heard it that it was the perfect summation of her experience on the cruise. "Therefore, if anyone is in Christ, he is a new creation; the old has gone, the new has come!"

❧

By late afternoon, Laura was comfortably wedged between Graham and Kathi, thousands of feet in the air, soaring towards home. In order for the three of them to travel together, Graham had had to forfeit his seat in first class at the cost of his comfort. Even in the aisle seat, there was precious little leg room, and he spent the majority of the flight seeking a position that would allow full circulation to his lower extremities.

Kathi, who sat by the window, spent the first 30 minutes of the flight crying softly, an extension of her tearful farewell with Jack on the ship.

"We were so in love," she lamented tearfully. "I'll never find another man to take his place."

A passing flight attendant noticed her distress and handed her a box of tissues. A few minutes later, he was back, "Feeling any better? Is there something I can get for you?"

Kathi looked up at the sound of his voice, noticing for the first time that this solicitous attendant was male, and very good looking, too. A bright smile flashed across her tear-streaked face. "I'm feeling much better thank you. Although, now that you mention it, I could use a little company to help cheer me up. Do you have a minute? Being a flight attendant must be so exciting. I've always been fascinated by air travel."

Laura rolled her eyes in amused exasperation as she saw the young man eagerly take the bait, and Graham, seeing Laura's look and recognizing Kathi's tactics, chuckled deeply.

❧

Howard Wells stood at the gate, anxiously studying the passengers as they disembarked from the plane.

"Where could they be?" he muttered as the steady flow of exiting passengers reduced to a trickle. "Graham should be off by now, he had a seat in first class."

A worrying thought struck him. Suppose they missed the plane. Suppose there was an accident and the three of them were at a hospital in Miami. He paced back and forth before the gate. When a group of flight attendants finally emerged from the plane, signaling that the passengers were unloaded, Howard became truly fearful. Something was wrong.

He had moved forward to question one of the stewardesses when he caught sight of a dark haired young woman dressed from head to toe in eye-catching fuchsia being escorted off the plane on the arm of a handsome flight attendant. He breathed a sigh of relief. Everything there was business as usual. "Kathi!" He raised a hand in greeting and stopped, his arm frozen in midair as he saw Laura and Graham step from the plane.

He stood transfixed as he watched the statuesque beauty move toward him. *She looks more like her mother than ever,* he thought with pride, *a classic beauty, poised and elegant in her navy suit.* But something was different. *Perhaps it is her tan or her sun streaked hair,* he mused. Her hair. That was it. She was wearing it down, a style she hadn't worn in years.

By now, Laura had spotted her father and was hurrying toward him, with Graham following in her wake.

That's when he saw it. The change wasn't her tan or her hairstyle. It was her eyes. Gone was the guarded expression that had haunted those dark eyes for so many lonely years. Today, the velvety brown eyes he loved so dearly were shining brightly, reflecting the same smile that lit up her face.

Howard's heart leaped. *Could it be?* Had his fervent prayers finally been answered? Was it possible she had received the message of comfort and hope that he so longed to share? He looked past his daughter to the face of his trusted friend, his eyes seeking an answer to his unspoken question. Graham nodded slowly, a broad smile stealing across his face.

In seconds, father and daughter were locked in a tearful embrace. "Oh, Lynn," Howard whispered, "Our baby has come home."

epilogue

Laura stared unseeing across the cruise ship's crowded, candlelit dining room as myriad thoughts vied for her attention. So much had happened in the last six months, there had been little time for the introspective inventory that she paused now to take.

I am a working woman now, she thought with pride, successfully integrated into the accounting team at Cunningham and Associates. She loved her job, the work was challenging, and the people were supportive. In fact, she almost felt guilty for collecting a paycheck for doing something so enjoyable.

At home, her relationship with her father had blossomed. Together, in quiet moments stolen from their busy schedules, they were rebuilding the friendship they had once shared, relearning the reasons they loved one another.

With the unlimited demands on her time, Laura had learned quickly to prioritize her life. She found that by placing her heavenly Father first, all other things fell into much better alignment.

Kathi and she joined a church and were actively involved in a women's Bible study that met on Tuesday nights. Laura smiled. Kathi was especially active in the church now that she was dating the handsome new pastor of the singles group.

But in Laura's mind, infinitely sweeter was the time that she spent alone with God, either reading her Bible or in prayer. Those daily visits provided the solid foundation she needed on which to build her life. She had grown to love and cherish Him and in turn, His peace and joy permeated every area of her life.

Her gaze drifted down to the sparkling sapphire ring on her left hand and the slender gold band that gleamed beside it, reminding her of the most recent change in her life, one whose impact she had just begun to appreciate.

Laura looked up into the smoky gray gaze of the man she'd

vowed to love forever. *That shouldn't be too difficult,* she thought with a grin as she studied his handsome face. Graham smiled warmly at her, that same heart-stopping, knee-weakening smile that she loved, and he reached across the table to rest his hand on hers.

Her husband. The man that she had come to love and respect over the last six months was now hers in every way. Yesterday, in a lovely ceremony before family and friends, they had been joined together in holy matrimony. They shared so much intellectually, emotionally, and spiritually, and finally, last night, physically. Laura flushed at the memory of her wondrous initiation into the fullness of marriage.

"What do you think, Mrs. Kirkland?"

Laura started in surprise at the sound of the voice. Reluctantly, she emerged from her daydreams and turned to face the man seated beside her. "I beg your pardon?"

"I didn't think you heard me." Mr. Bowden, their table companion, smiled patiently. "I asked if you and your husband would care to join us at the theater this evening? I hear the show is marvelous."

Laura gave him a polite smile. "That sounds great. We'd..." She was silenced by the sudden squeeze of her hand.

"What my wife is trying to say is that you're right, the show sounds great," Graham continued for her, "however, we won't be able to join you, I'm afraid." He patted Laura's hand. "Mrs. Kirkland and I have had a very big day and plan to retire early."

Mr. Bowden missed the bewildered look on Laura's face as he and his wife stood to leave. "I understand," he said with a nod. "I feel the same way when I travel. Good night then. See you tomorrow." The two of them headed for the exit.

Laura turned an astonished look on Graham. Once the Bowdens were out of earshot, she asked, "Big day? Since when does lying around a pool on a cruise ship all day constitute a big day?" She shook her head in bewilderment. "I thought you wanted to see the show."

"I happen to know that they are repeating the performance tomorrow at three." He stood up and moved slowly around the table toward Laura, a wicked grin playing across his face. "As for tonight," his deep voice was silky smooth, "I thought perhaps you'd like. . ." he leaned over and whispered something in her ear.

Laura blushed prettily and nodded. She stood to join him, and the two of them strolled arm in arm from the dining room, well on their way to happily ever after.

A Letter To Our Readers

Dear Reader:

In order that we might better contribute to your reading enjoyment, we would appreciate your taking a few minutes to respond to the following questions. When completed, please return to the following:

Rebecca Germany, Editor
Heartsong Presents
P.O. Box 719
Uhrichsville, Ohio 44683

1. Did you enjoy reading *A Change of Heart*?
   ❑ Very much. I would like to see more books
      by this author!
   ❑ Moderately
      I would have enjoyed it more if _____

   _____

2. Are you a member of *Heartsong Presents*? Yes   No
   If no, where did you purchase this book? _____

   _____

3. What influenced your decision to purchase this
   book? (Check those that apply.)

   ❑ Cover   ❑ Back cover copy

   ❑ Title   ❑ Friends

   ❑ Publicity   ❑ Other _____

4. On a scale from 1 (poor) to 10 (superior), please rate the following elements.

    ___Heroine   ___Plot

    ___Hero   ___Inspirational theme

    ___Setting   ___Secondary characters

5. What settings would you like to see covered in *Heartsong Presents* books?

    _____

    _____

6. What are some inspirational themes you would like to see treated in future books?_____

    _____

    _____

7. Would you be interested in reading other *Heartsong Presents* titles?   ❑ Yes   ❑ No

8. Please check your age range:
  ❑ Under 18   ❑ 18-24   ❑ 25-34
  ❑ 35-45   ❑ 46-55   ❑ Over 55

9. How many hours per week do you read? ———

Name _____

Occupation _____

Address _____

City _____ State _____ Zip _____

Introducing New Authors!

___**Rae Simons**—*The Quiet Heart*—Thrilled at the opportunity to work near Liam, the love of her life, Dorrie has accepted a teaching position in a school for troubled children. Dorrie is desperate to please Liam and be the person he thinks she is. Will Dorrie ever possess a quiet heart? HP114 $2.95

___**Birdie L. Etchison**—*The Heart Has Its Reasons*—Emily, the simple Quaker, wants only a simple life. But things get complicated when her dashing friend introduces her to handsome Ben Galloway. As she sorts through her conflicting emotions, Emily finds that love and commitment are anything but simple decisions. HP123 $2.95

___**Mary LaPietra**—*His Name on Her Heart*—Marnette is haunted by her past. As God's plan unfolds, Marnette finds herself living with previously unknown relatives in the newly settled prairie. Although she constructs a tissue of lies about her past, Marnette is not as successful in denying her attraction to Drew Britton. HP124 $2.95

___**Elizabeth Murphey**—*Love's Tender Gift*—Determined to prove herself to Joel, Val decides to infiltrate a local cult as a class project. But she isn't prepared for her own vulnerability to the persuasive tactics of the cult. With Val's life in danger, Joel follows her to Ireland where she has been lured by promises of eternal life and love. Will Joel find Val in time to convince her that she already has his love...and God's? HP125 $2.95

······Heart♥ng ······

Hearts♥ng Presents
Love Stories Are Rated G!

That's for godly, gratifying, and of course, great! If you love a thrilling love story, but don't appreciate the sordidness of popular paperback romances, **Heartsong Presents** is for you. In fact, **Heartsong Presents** is the *only inspirational romance book club*, the only one featuring love stories where Christian faith is the primary ingredient in a marriage relationship.

Sign up today to receive your first set of four, never before published Christian romances. Send no money now; you will receive a bill with the first shipment. You may cancel at any time without obligation, and if you aren't completely satisfied with any selection, you may return the books for an immediate refund!

Imagine. . .four new romances every month—two historical, two contemporary—with men and women like you who long to meet the one God has chosen as the love of their lives. . .all for the low price of $9.97 postpaid.

To join, simply complete the coupon below and mail to the address provided. **Heartsong Presents** romances are rated G for another reason: They'll arrive *Godspeed!*
